CW00500014

WARRIOR WITCH

THE CURSED COVEN OF SPELLS HOLLOW

BOOK ONE

TL HAMILTON

KATHERINE ISAAC

NIGHTSHADE PUBLISHING

Cover Art by JodieLocks Designs.

Map by DAZED Designs.

Editing by Kaye Kemp Book Polishing.

Part of the shared world The Cursed Coven of Spells Hollow, brought to you by Nightshade Publishing.

www.tlhamiltonauthor.com

www.katherineisaac.com

Warrior Witch Playlist

Baby Outlaw - Elle King
Ignorance - Paramore
Oh No! - MARINA
Toxic - Lauren Babic
Witching Hour - In This Moment
Kill The Lights - The Birthday Massacre
Fire Fire - Flyleaf
Vicious - Halestorm
Boys Wanna Fight - Garbage
Bitch - Meredith Brooks

Find the whole Playlist here:

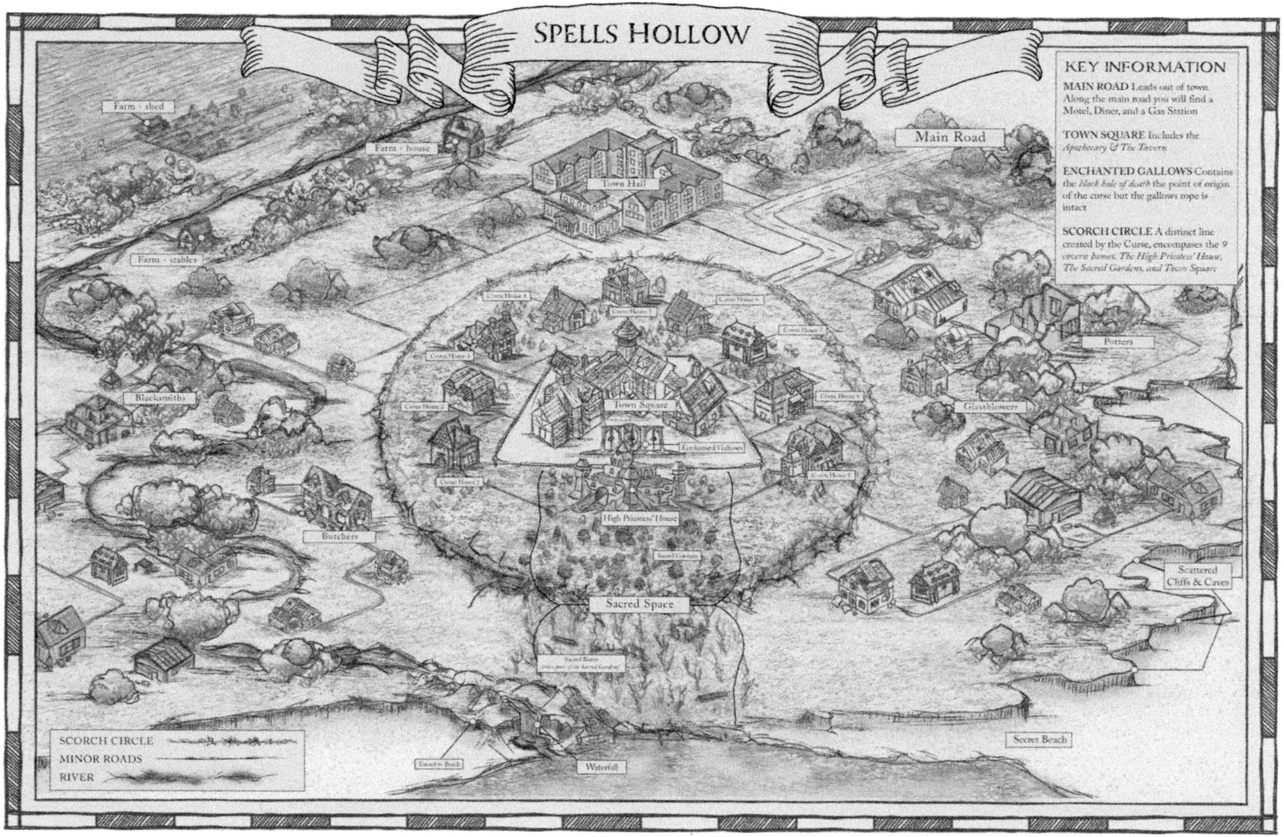
SPELLS HOLLOW
KEY INFORMATION
MAIN ROAD Leads out of town. Along the main road you will find a Motel, Diner, and a Gas Station
TOWN SQUARE Includes the *Apothecary & The Tavern*
ENCHANTED GALLOWS Contains the *black hole of death* the point of origin of the curse but the gallows rope is intact
SCORCH CIRCLE A distinct line created by the Curse, encompases the 9 *coven homes. The High Priestess' House, The Sacred Gardens, and Town Square*
Farm - shed
Farm - house
Farm - stables
Town Hall
Main Road
Blacksmiths
Butchers
Town Square
Enchanted Gallows
High Priestess' House
Sacred Gardens
Sacred Space
Potters
Glassblowers
Scattered Cliffs & Caves
Secret Beach
Waterfall
SCORCH CIRCLE
MINOR ROADS
RIVER

To the children determined to read over our shoulders.
Back it up.
Mummy's writing sex scenes.

Harlow

"It was a compliment!" I insisted as another punch breezed past my nose. "Didn't you hear me? I said it was *impressive* that your girlfriend can look past your scraggly muttonchop sideburns and see the three struggling brain cells you call a personality. True love really does exist! You two are an inspiration."

The man huffed an angry breath, his bright red cheeks almost steaming with rage. "Mouthy bitch!"

He threw another punch, but his movements were slow and easy to avoid.

"Sir, please, keep your arms at your sides! Unlike your girlfriend, I'm not prepared to handle your eye-watering odor."

Riling him up probably wasn't the best idea, but it was just too easy. Not to mention, fun.

Growling, he swung for me again, not noticing the wall directly behind me until I dashed to the side. The painful crunch of his knuckles against the bricks echoed in my ears, and I almost felt bad for the guy. Though at least he wouldn't be using that hand to grope unsuspecting strangers on the dance floor again any time soon.

Heels clacked on the concrete, then a shrill voice yelled, “Kevy-Bear!”

Girlfriend finally finished flirting at the bar, I see.

“Fuck off, Sandra!” He pushed her away roughly with his good hand, turning to me with a snarl. “This bitch is gonna—”

Blood spurted from his nostrils like juice from a crushed watermelon as I introduced his nose to my fist.

I had no desire to hear the rest of that bastard’s threat.

His head smacked back on the wall with a resounding crack that had the people surrounding us cringing in sympathy. A group of men wearing matching leather vests pushed through the crowd to where ‘Kevy-Bear’ lay in a pathetic, bloody, crumpled ball. Served him right.

“You and your little boy band are formally banned from Cassandra’s Bane,” I announced, wiping the asshole’s blood on the side of my dark work pants. “Now get out of here before we call the cops.”

The men exchanged glances before scampering, cussing me out as they dragged the heap of flesh I assumed was their boss. “You won’t get away with this!”

“Take care, Kevy-Bear!” I yelled after them, waving my fingers delicately, like I hadn’t just knocked out a man twice my size.

I was always happy to throw out rowdy customers. The other members of the security team at Cassandra’s Bane preferred to use their words and impressive physiques to intimidate people into leaving, but they were mostly men with several inches of height on me. At five-seven, I wasn’t short, but it wasn’t always easy to encourage people to kindly get the fuck out without making a few threats.

And if I had to make good on those threats, that was more than fine with me.

The crowd dispersed until only a small queue remained, so

I headed back inside the club to let the manager know the Grim Hearts MC members were acting up again. Something must have changed with them, because they never used to be this dickish. Not until recently. Now I had to throw out one or more of their members every other night.

Electricity crackled across my reddened knuckles with every step. I hadn't needed to use my magic in that fight, and now it was searching for a way out. I shook my hands to ease the stinging, and the sparks fizzled out. Still, the restless sensation in my body remained.

I shouldn't have finished off that asshole so quickly.

Just a few months ago, a fight like that would have left me relaxed and satisfied for a week, maybe more. Tonight, it barely scratched the surface of my tension.

"Kedron's not gonna be happy with you," my favorite voice sang from behind the bar.

Lindsay's golden makeup was almost dazzling under the flashing club lights. He was so beautiful it was no wonder he had so many regulars coming back here several times a week just to see him.

I'd known Lindsay since we were five years old when Alice fucking Presley—who thought she was so cool sharing a name with some king from like a hundred years ago, news flash, we were all orphans in that foster home—thought it would be funny to lock me in a closet with him after we'd switched the only clothes bought for us. Real original. Her laughter stopped real quick after I shaved one of her eyebrows off that night and Lindsay bleached the other.

We didn't last long in that home, or any home, but we'd bonded over revenge and a love of post-mayhem peanuts. Seventeen years later, my bestie still had my back.

"Kedron can smile and thank me." I stalked over to an empty corner of the bar, trying not to think about how much our boss will hate finding out about another fight at his venue. "Those jackasses had it coming, and you know it."

Lindsay nodded as he wiped down the bar, looking busy while we talked. "Oh, couldn't agree more there. But if you keep throwing out all our customers, even just the jackasses, there won't be any money coming in for us to get paid."

He had a point. That said, I wasn't about to let some scumbag carry on groping people under my watch. The people coming here had a right to safety, and I planned to earn my minimum wage paycheck.

"We need the money, Harlow," he reminded me, a serious tone smothering his usually light demeanor. "We can pick up extra shifts at Eclipse, no problem, but if you get any more medical bills because of a dumb fight—"

"I'm fine," I snap, leaving no room for arguments. "Now, is he in his office? I've gotta tell him about the MC."

He waved me off with one hand. "Don't worry about it. I'll go talk to him. He likes me better than you, anyway."

"You don't have to do that."

"Relax, Harlow. Think of it less as me cleaning up your mess and more of me seeking out angry office sex."

He bounced his eyebrows at me, throwing in a little shimmy until I cracked a reluctant grin.

"Slut," I murmured, unable to resist the olive branch.

"You know it. Now go cool off for ten out the back while I selflessly throw myself on Kedron's dick... I mean mercy."

Rolling my eyes at my thirsty bestie, I stalked across the floor, ignoring the panicked looks I received from patrons as they scurried out of my path. Beneath my skin, my veins buzzed with power that was unhappy with the brevity of the fight. It wanted out. Like a wayward puppy, a small current leaked from my fingertips and zapped a burly mountain of a man standing in front of the back door. With an undignified squeal, he turned, a wicked scowl morphing into something much more contrite as he shuffled aside so I could make my escape.

"Think grounding thoughts," I muttered, slamming the door behind me and resting against the brick exterior of the club.

I breathed in deeply, let it out, and growled as the urge to explode sent tremors through my limbs. Crossing the narrow alley to the building next door, I reared back and threw my whole body into a punch that lit up the darkness. Bright blue bolts of energy spider-webbed across the brick facade, leaving char marks in their wake. As the force of the blow crackled out, I folded forward, breathing hard.

"Shit." Blood leaked from my scratched-up knuckles, adding to the stains left by Kevy-Bear's nose as my heart hammered from the exertion of releasing that much power at once. Yet still, I twitched with more energy.

I'd rather fund Lindsay's makeup habit for a year than admit it, but I may have had a slight, barely there concern about the way the power thrumming in my veins seemed to have amplified over the last few months.

I flinched as a cold drop of water pinged off the tip of my nose and craned my neck to see clouds gathering in the previously clear night sky. My hair lifted in a sudden breeze, and I rubbed absently at the back of my neck. Goosebumps prickled across my skin as my instincts screamed at me that I was no longer alone in the alley. Whipping around, I tried to take on the entire dark space in one glance as several more raindrops bounced off my head.

"Who's there?" I called, raising my fists and almost smiling at the blue sparks that crackled over my bloody knuckles.

Nothing moved in the darkness, and after a few long minutes of quiet, I slowly relaxed out of my fighting stance, chuckling at myself. Maybe paranoia was the latest symptom of my growing power.

Cursing softly, I headed back toward the fire door. There were only three hours left of my shift, and I'd already been gone long enough that patrons could have caused trouble.

With one hand on the door, I took a bracing breath and paused as a shadow flitted across the painted wooden surface in front of me. Turning, I caught a flash of white fur disappearing at the end of the alley and immediately felt ridiculous.

It was just a stray dog.

Christ. Maybe I needed a holiday. Somewhere hot and sunny, far away from this rainy craphole of a city.

I looked up to gauge the progress of the storm and froze at the sight of a sky full of stars.

Not a cloud in sight.

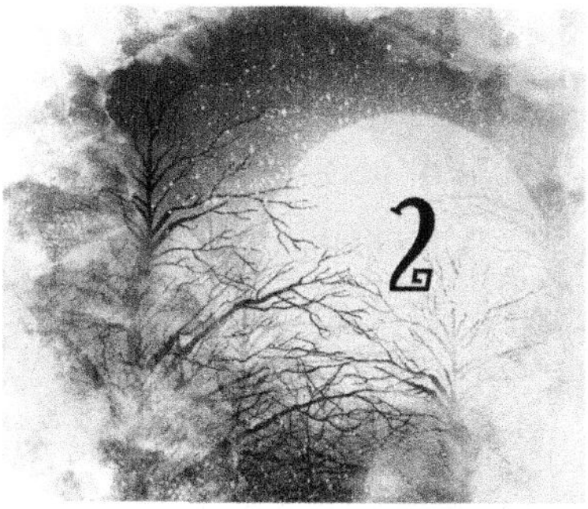

Harlow

THE INCESSANT CHIRPING of birds outside my window woke me far too early the next morning. My fingers tingled with the need to lash out with just a little power to make them shut the hell up. At least for another five minutes.

Kedron held me back after closing to strongly suggest I refrain from shedding further blood under his roof. Apparently, pointing out that blood wasn't technically shed until we were outside—therefore not under his roof—wasn't the response he wanted, and my penance had been an even longer lecture with frequent threats to my job security. Just another Thursday night, really. His reaction probably would have been worse if Lindsay hadn't spent half his bar shift on his knees.

Gods bless my horny hero.

By the time I had sufficiently pandered to Kedron's need for order and done a last sweep of the bathrooms and dark corners for those too busy hooking up to take the hint and move the hell on, dawn was on the horizon and my head felt it weighed a thousand pounds. Between the late night and the hangover from the amount of power I discharged, I had flopped into bed and blacked out until Tweety Mc-soon-to-be KFC started his racket. Flexing my knuckles, I tried to remind myself that electrocuting the local fauna in a sleep-deprived rage was probably not the best way to start the day.

I could do this. I'd just ignore the piercing call that seemed to have been picked up by a new group of flying rats and...

A clash of metal on stone sent my heart into my throat as I bolted out of bed, ready to defend my apartment from intruders.

"My bad."

Shit. Addie was trying to cook again.

With a last desperate look at the pile of pillows and blankets that begged for my return, I heaved a sigh and went in search of my little protégé.

"Addison Mae, what the fuck are you doing here at this hour?" I asked, leaning a hip on the kitchen counter and taking in the sight of the little ingrate.

Five-foot nothing, with dirty blonde hair and the biggest blue eyes—which she used to best effect whenever she needed something—Addie was a product of the same orphanage that spat out Lindsay and me, a decade ago. Meaning she was smart as anything, a boss at manipulation, and used to fighting for what she wanted.

"I was hungry. It's the end of the month, and they're cutting costs, which means the food is shit until they sell the next kid."

I rolled my eyes at her dramatics and switched off the burner on the stove.

"So you thought you'd come and burn my place down instead?"

Her lips twitched, trying to suppress a wicked smile. "It's your own fault for hiding the spare key in the dumbest place possible. For someone in security, you're pretty lax around here."

"That's because anyone stupid enough to break in gets zapped."

I chuckled to myself at the memory of the last guy who tried. Only things he left with were an eyeful of Lindsay walking around nude, fresh out the shower, and a painful-looking twitch.

"Wish I could zap away the people I don't like. All I've got is the pepper spray you got me for my birthday."

While Addie was technically a witch, same as Lindsay and me, she'd never been able to access her magic. We could sense it in her, but for some strange reason... nothing. And unfortunately, potential adoptive parents weren't willing to take a chance on a "broken" witch.

Lucky for her, Lindsay and I had a soft spot for rebellious freaks.

"We'll level you up to a taser for your eighteenth," I promised.

It wouldn't be difficult to get her the taser now if I really thought about it. But she'd already pepper sprayed two other teens in the foster program for pouring a bucket of ice water on her while she slept—got 'em right in the eyes, I was so proud—and I wasn't totally convinced she wouldn't tase them for the same offense. Better to wait just a few more years.

Turning away from the would-be cooking disaster surrounding the stove, I pulled a box of cereal from the cupboard and filled up two bowls.

"Seriously? I wanted to make waffles." Addie pouted, giving me her best doe-eyes.

"It's the end of the month here, too, kid. At least this has real sugar." I grabbed the milk and topped off our breakfasts. "Pick whatever you want on the TV and let's eat. If I have to be up at this hour, I at least wanna be fed."

Addie pulled two spoons from the drawer and dunked

them in the bowls—her version of contributing to the meal. "I can work with that."

***

The minutes before opening were some of my favorites at work. The air smelled like lemon from the surface spray used to clean down the bar and tables, and the dance floor shone with polish, clean—for now—of the sticky alcohol that would mar the surface and suction shoes come closing. Outside, the queue of partiers awaiting their first drinks buzzed with excitement, their voices muted by thick walls for the moment, but that would change very soon. I took a deep breath and smiled. This was the quiet before the storm. And I lived for the storm.

"One minute until the doors open. All staff confirm you're ready, bitches." Lindsay's voice crackled through my earpiece, sounding as official as he ever did. I rolled my eyes and added my own "ready" to the chorus of responses.

Power crackled through my veins, lifting the hair on my arms as the first patrons trickled in and bee-lined to the bar for their first round. Kedron would get his panties in a twist if I got in a knock-down-drag-out fight two nights in a row, but it didn't stop me hoping someone would give me a reason to work out some of this excess energy.

I got my wish three hours later.

"Harlow, I gotta go on my break. Can you cover the door for me?"

A glance at my watch told me it was around about the time Benji's kid went to bed, so rather than give him shit for handballing his time on the door, I weaved through the mass of sweating bodies and broke out into the night to see a sheepish-looking Benji with his cell already in hand.

The guy may have been half giant, but he had the softest

heart of anyone I'd ever met. Especially when it came to his family.

"I owe you one."

"Say goodnight to Jesse for me." I gave him a half smile before resuming my best sneer to welcome the preppy douche crew who had stepped up to the entrance.

"Is this really necessary?" Chad #1 asked as he fished his Hermes wallet out of his Prada slacks.

"Not at all. You're free to fuck off and not waste my time."

Chad #2 smirked at me, holding out a crisp twenty dollar note. "How about we skip all of these formalities, and you just step aside, sweetheart."

I crossed my arms over my chest and took a lean against the doorframe.

"Tell me, Chad—"

"My name's not Chad."

"Do you like your balls, Chad?"

Chad #2 frowned as though I'd given him the sphinx's riddle to solve.

"What—?"

I lifted a hand and let a line of electricity dance across my fingertips.

"Because I have a policy. If an asshole calls me sweetheart, I surgically remove the contents of his sack. Don't worry, it's completely non-invasive, and has a one hundred percent success rate in ensuring complete sterilization so that there's no next gen douchebags coming from your line."

Chad #2's Andrew Jackson sagged in his hand in much the same way I imagined his limp dick sagged at the hooting and hollering of his boys in response to my very earnest offer. His eyes flashed yellow briefly before he backed up to a safe distance.

"Screw you, bitch. You couldn't handle this."

Oh look, he was grabbing the less-than-a-handful that was his junk.

"Come on, boys, this place sucks, anyway."

As the Chad brigade moved off down the road, they continued to vocalize their dislike of Cassandra's Bane.

Fucking idiots.

"Fucking idiots." The deep chuckle that followed the statement washed over me like bathwater. Warm and sensual, I felt the urge to melt into the body beside me. He smelled of petrichor, of earth and ozone and the promise of cleansing rain, and a smile hitched the corner of my mouth a moment before I felt the pinch of a blade at my back.

"Cute party trick, but now we need to have a chat, you and me."

Motherfucker. How dare he interrupt my attraction by being... from the corner of my eye, I caught a familiar patch on his leather jacket and barely suppressed a sigh. If it wasn't the consequences of my own actions. Looked like Kevy-bear held a grudge.

"Walk. Around the corner, and don't try anything funny if you want to keep your insides on the inside."

I turned my eyes to the overcast sky and decided to play along for now. I was hilarious, damn it, and best believe I was fully capable of looking after my own insides. Aaand now the word inside had lost all meaning. Great.

Stumbling around the corner and into the alley that still bore the black marks of my power discharge from the night before, I found the nice-smelling jerk had brought friends.

"Hello, boys," I called, ignoring the sharp implement digging into my skin.

As one, the group glowered at me like I'd hurt their leader. Oh...wait.

The guy behind me finally retracted the stupid knife, and I

got my first good look at him. Dark hair, darker eyes, and a delicious number of tattoos.

Bad Harlow. Stop ogling the bad guy. Focus on something else until you fry the bastards.

Looking around the small group, something occurred to me, and I couldn't suppress my gasp of delight.

"Oh my gods. Do you guys all have matching clothes? Like... did someone have to put in an order so you could all wear the same thing? That's so cute! It has your little logo on it, too!"

"Shut it, witch," a beefy blonde guy growled from the back of his motorbike.

"I'm sorry, but like, did someone do it on Canva? Or did you have to send away to some other company to..." My taunt fizzled out as the clouds parted and Bike Boy's blonde hair shifted to a blood red.

"Witch."

The whisper floated through the alley, and without conscious thought, my head dropped back and my eyes focused on the largest blood moon I'd ever seen.

In an instant, my body seized. Every muscle turning to stone as the moon expanded, flooding my vision so that all I could see, all I knew, was the deep, viscous red.

"Little lightning rod, your time is as short as your temper. Seek your salvation in Spells Hollow."

The voice reached for me through the moon's powerful pull. Like an anchor, I wanted to reach back. It sounded female. Warm and tinged with an affection that was almost as confusing as the message, it carried a weight to it that was almost physical. Authoritative. I took a step forward, and as though the loss of paralysis broke the spell, the red drained from my vision, and I sagged like a marionette with its strings cut.

Awareness returned slowly as I registered the cool night air, followed by...

"Motherf—"

Pain radiated through my cheek, and I blinked hard to focus on the beefy blonde asshole who was rearing back for a second shot.

"Playtime's over, assholes." No longer in the mood to entertain, I gathered my power, ready to let loose.

The fire exit beside us blew open to reveal Lindsay's favorite Mr. Tall, Hung (his words, not mine) and Extremely Pissed Off.

"What the fuck do you think you're doing?" Kedron glowered at the group of us like we were teen miscreants caught smoking behind the school bleachers.

"This has nothing to do with—"

My boss kept talking at me as though the blonde idiot didn't exist.

"I've told you before. Kick these guy's asses on your own time. While you're here, you're mine. Get back to work."

"But I was just gonna—"

"No."

Spoilsport.

Pouting at Kedron for ruining my fun, I shouldered past the pretty psycho behind me who was too busy frowning at the sky to notice my departure and headed back toward the front of the establishment.

Seek your salvation in Spells Hollow.

I paused, wondering if the echo came on the wind, or if it had tunneled into my subconscious. Either way, it didn't matter. Salvation was for those looking to be saved.

"And my life is fucking peachy just the way it is," I muttered, lifting my chin at Benji and striding back inside to greet the chaos.

Harlow

I TRIED to stay close to the main dance floor through my shift for two reasons; first, it was my job. Duh. The dance floor was where all the action was, and a third lecture from Kedron within a day didn't sound appetizing.

Second, I was a lot less likely to get a repeat of the knife-to-the-back trick if I stayed indoors. No matter how much I enjoyed a good fight—or how lickable that MC psycho's tattoos were—knife play wasn't on my kink list.

A restless energy pulsed through me as I slowly circled the crowds. My eyes darted around the room, unable to concentrate on anything for more than a second, until my gaze settled on the direction of the exit. I forced myself to keep walking, desperately trying to shake the strange feeling. Each step away felt wrong somehow. Like at any moment, I'd be scolded by a teacher for breaking some arbitrary rule I never cared to learn.

Positioning myself against a wall, facing the crowd with the exit behind them, the feeling faded into something more comfortable. I stood there, pretending to watch over the dancing patrons, and the pounding bass faded into the background until the only sound in my mind was the voice from earlier.

Your time is as short as your temper.

Rude. What the hell was I supposed to do with that?

Slipping my cell out of my pocket, I did a quick search on Spells Hollow. The first result was some new age gemstone store in Delaware, followed by some tourist attraction in Dublin.

Please tell me the moon doesn't want me to go overseas.

At the bottom of the page was a Reddit thread on local legends and urban explorer locations. Four hours away near New York was a town rumored to be deserted, and infamous in certain circles for being home to a broken coven.

Shoving the device back in my pocket, I scanned the room for trouble.

This was what I did. No weird ass vision was going to send me on a wild goose chase across the state.

I'd probably just had a seizure, brought on by my increasingly unstable magic... or something.

That moon had been something else, though. I'd probably understand what it meant if I'd had a traditional coven upbringing. Instead, I watched as witches filled the club, freshly energized from their full moon rituals. High on the connection to their magic, rather than fighting daily to stay in control.

Maybe I should encourage Addie to find a youth coven or something. Could they help her unlock her magic?

A tap on my shoulder snapped me out of my thoughts, and music flooded my ears again. I blinked up at Lindsay's glittering face as he motioned for me to follow him to the bar's storeroom.

He hopped around some boxes to the back of the room,

calling back to me, "You looked serious back there! Did something happen?"

I leaned against the door with a sigh. "I was just thinking. Do we need some witch friends?"

His head popped up, one sparkling eyebrow raised. "We have witch friends."

"We have work friends who are witches. Huge difference."

"What's brought this on?" he asked as he started loading up my arms with bottles. "Got some full moon FOMO?"

"Something like that." I shrugged, careful of the hoard of alcohol in my arms. "It's probably nothing. Just been a long, weird night."

"I think you could use a day off," he said, picking up his own box of goodies for the bar. "Come on, help me restock, then we'll grab a quick drink before we get back to it. In a few more hours, we'll be back home without a care in the world."

I followed him back to the bar, muttering under my breath, "That last part seems optimistic..."

Benji's voice mumbled through my earpiece that we were now at capacity for the night, and it showed in the crowd surrounding the bar. Lindsay's team were handling them with ease, ever the professionals, as they racked up their tips, and I did my best to stay out of their way while assisting my bestie.

As the music's tempo picked up into the remix of some new supe band—I vaguely recognized it as something Addie had tried to get me into while driving her around—Lindsay pulled me over to the corner out of the view of security cameras. He shoved a shot glass into my hand and clinked it with his matching one.

"Just a quick one to get us through," he yelled over the music, then knocked back his drink in a swift gulp.

I looked down into the shot, twisting the glass back and forth and watching the small ripples on the tequila's surface.

Maybe a little alcohol would pull me out of my head. A blinding green laser flashed over my vision, momentarily stunning me as the club's lights morphed from yellow to red. The color seeped through the shot in my hand, and suddenly it wasn't alcohol, but a blood red warning. Flinching hard, the glass dropped from my lax fingers and shattered at my feet, sending glass and tequila across the floorboards.

I cursed, trying half-heartedly to shake the liquid from the toe of my boot.

"Right, that's it. Come with me."

With a far steadier hand than mine, Lindsay steered me back into the storeroom and over to a keg to sit.

"You've been skittish for the last few hours, then the FOMO stuff, and now you're wasting good alcohol? What gives?"

I smirked at him, ready to make a joke about wasted alcohol, but the look on his face made me pause. Genuine concern shone in his eyes as he lowered himself to a crouch.

"Talk to me, Harls. Something's going on with you, and I know it's more than getting jumped by those biker morons earlier."

"How...? Kedron." I should have been pissed about our boss getting into my personal business, but I could admit it was kind of his business, too, when it happened on his property. Plus, I'd been sharing my shit with Lindsay since I was old enough to be getting into it. He deserved an explanation.

"Look. This...whatever it is. Funk, maybe? That I'm in has nothing to do with the leathered stooges from earlier. They just happened to be present for the event." I took a deep breath. "I had a vision tonight."

The room vibrated to the bass of the music thumping through the club, but the storeroom remained silent as I waited for Lindsay to... laugh? Tell me I was losing my mind? I wasn't sure what I expected, but as my opinionated bestie kept his mouth shut and waited for details I didn't think he'd want, I wasn't sure how to elaborate.

Power began to crawl beneath my skin, reacting to my discomfort as though it were a threat. Shit. That was the last thing I needed right now.

"Will you please say something?" I asked, lashing out with words to try to stem the tide of my power.

"I'm waiting to hear what has you so worked up. You had a vision. You're a witch. It can come with the territory. So what about this vision has you looking ready to bolt outta here?"

Best friends are meant to call you on your shit, I reminded myself as I forced another deep breath and ordered my muscles to relax. I even tried for a smile, but if his raised eyebrow was any indication, I might have just looked constipated.

"It was the usual. Go here or you'll die. No biggie. You're right. If I'd grown up in a coven, I'd probably know all about the correct response to visions."

Lindsay's face softened. "We're our own coven, you, me, even Addie. Chosen family, babe. Now, where do we have to go to keep you whole?"

"Nowhere."

"Harlow."

I surged to my feet, restless energy flooding me despite my attempt at keeping zen. Let's face it, it was always a losing fight. I couldn't drag Lindsay into this shit. I didn't even want to be in it.

"No. I don't care what the moon says. We're not going."

"Yes, we are. I'll go to the end of the world to save your cute butt. Now give me a direction."

"No way, bitch. You don't run upstairs when the killer is in the house, and you don't road trip to a creepy ass town in the middle of nowhere because a creepy ass psychic voice tells you to. You'll. End. Up. Dead!"

"You'll be dead, anyway!"

Lindsay's shout interrupted my rant and shocked me into taking a proper look at my best friend. Beneath his makeup, his skin had paled, and his eyes shone a little too much in the dim light as his chest heaved with suppressed emotion.

"I can't lose you. Ride or die, baby. Now, please, tell me where we're going."

"Spells Hollow."

Lindsay and I both jumped, turning guiltily to find our boss leaning in the doorway.

"I'll make this easy on you," he continued, moving into the space and standing close to Lindsay. Like iron to a magnet, my bestie leaned toward Kedron, drawing comfort from his mere presence.

"You're fired."

"You can't do that." The words were out of my mouth before I'd even processed what he said.

He very much could do that, and would be right to, with the trouble that I'd brought to his door in the last couple of nights. The problem was, without the club, I didn't know what I would do. Work, fight, sleep, repeat had been my life for the last few years. I was happy with that.

Kedron shook his head as though he could follow my thoughts. Hell, maybe he could. There was a lot about my boss that was still a mystery to me, and he sure knew a hell of a lot more than he should about—

"How do you know about Spells Hollow?"

"It's what I do. I sell booze, and I know things."

I flipped him off for the reference but couldn't suppress the hurt that lanced through me at being let go.

"This is for your own good, kid. It needs to happen. And you." He cupped Lindsay's jaw and pulled him in until their foreheads pressed together.

"Keep her safe and then come back to me. I know you need to do this, but I need you."

Lindsay closed his eyes and nodded, lifting his lips for a sweet kiss before Kedron broke away from him, leaving us to the silence of the storeroom, broken only by the bass from the dance floor beyond.

"That was intense. I thought you two were just casual," I said, hoping Lindsay would accept the change of subject so I could live in denial about my future for a moment more.

"Yeah. Me, too." His eyes stayed glued to the doorway as though hoping Kedron would reappear with more answers.

The seconds ticked by, and as the tempo of the bass shifted, signaling a new song, Lindsay shook himself. "Well, I guess we're off the clock now."

I snorted. "I don't know if you are. So far as I can tell, I'm the only one who got fired."

The pout he turned on me was ridiculous, and just the thing I needed to lift the funk that was settling on me.

And then he had to open his mouth.

"Suck it up, bitch. We're getting margaritas, then following your fucking destiny."

Harlow

"I HAVE A QUESTION FOR YOU, and I don't want you to think too long about it. Just go with your gut and spit out the answer that feels right." Addie flopped onto my bed beside the open suitcase I was staring into, contemplating life, the universe, and how I got into this mess.

I grunted, already knowing what my answer was regardless of what came out of her mouth next.

"Can I have a—"

"No."

"—dog?"

That was a new one.

"We don't need a pet. We have you." I ruffled her hair and chuckled at her scowl.

"Okay, so your gut sucks. Just think about it. Coming home from a long night and having a fluffy ball of loving fur to cuddle up with... Plus, he could totally keep me and the apartment safe while you and Lindsay work your crazy hours."

"You've been rehearsing this pitch for a while, haven't you?"

"I'm prepared to make an interactive presentation if you need more convincing."

Suddenly, the idea of road tripping into the unknown wasn't so terrifying. I started throwing any clean underwear I could find into the suitcase.

"Oh, come on!" Addie whined. "This dog is so cute, you'd love him! He's been walking around with me for days. One of those big, white, husky-looking things, but he's a total softy. Definitely a cuddler."

"Nope. Nothing you say will make me want some mutt in my apartment and definitely not in my bed."

"But I already named him."

"Addie."

"Fine." She sat up, watching closely as I moved to my closet and started pulling down jackets and shirts to pack.

"Where are you going, anyway?"

"Chasing destiny, apparently," I muttered, debating whether my old cardigan was a beneficial addition to the suitcase.

"Cool. When do we leave? We'll need to stop by the home for my stuff."

Shit. She wasn't going to like this. Tossing the cardigan in with my favorite pair of jeans, I dropped onto the bed beside her.

"We can't take you with us this time, Ads. Between the guys who threatened me last night and the sheer stupidity of following a vision to an abandoned town, it's just too dangerous."

Addie's eyes lit up, and I silently cursed myself for making the trip seem even more tempting.

"Whatever you're thinking, forget it. I'm serious, Addison. No."

"Ooh, you full-named me. I must be in real trouble."

The corner of my mouth twitched, but I refused to show her how much her theatrics amused me. She'd use the knowledge for evil, and I'd never have authority over her again.

"If you stay put, I'm prepared to have another conversation about the mutt when I get back." I wasn't going to mention the conversation would be a repeat of the one we'd just had. As in: never, ever will we keep a dog in the house. I'd use the leverage I had to keep her safe, though.

"Fine," she groaned, rolling off the bed and strolling to the door.

"Wait, where are you going?" I asked, feeling the need to repair the rift I suddenly felt open between us. Doubling back, she threw her arms around me in a quick but fierce hug.

"Go do your thing, and I'll do mine. See you soon, and don't die."

I hugged her back just as hard, resting my cheek on her hair.

"I won't if you don't. We'll be back before you know it. Love you, squirt."

"Love you, too."

***

The first hour of the "Epic Road Trip of Destiny"—as Lindsay insisted on naming it—went seamlessly. Lindsay played DJ in the passenger seat of our shared Toyota Camry while I steered us onto the highway and pointed us toward Spells freaking Hollow. It was as we hit the ninety-minute mark, things started to get weird.

"Can you hear that noise?" I asked as he changed up the Spotify playlist.

"What?"

I frowned in the rearview, trying to pinpoint where the knocking sound could be coming from. It wasn't the tires, and the doors were all firmly closed...

"I'm just going to pull over a minute. I think it's coming

from the trunk. You promised me you weren't bringing those stilettos, so if they're banging against something we need, I'm going to be pissed."

He sighed as I turned on my signal and pulled onto the side of the highway. "They're my lucky pair, but I left them at home; so whatever it is, it isn't my fault."

I rolled my eyes, climbing out of the car and circling around to the trunk, where the knocking continued.

"What the...?" Popping the lock, I sprung back as a small blonde stowaway burst out from between the baggage.

"Oh, thank the gods! I was worried you couldn't hear me, and I really need to pee."

Addie leaned her head outside the trunk, glancing around at all the pavement and not much else.

"Why the hell didn't you pull over at a rest stop? A gas station, maybe. I'm bursting here, Harls."

"Then I guess you're going on the side of the road," Lindsay said, leaning a hip on the back of my car.

"Ew, you heathen." Hoisting herself out of the trunk, she waved her hands in front of her, moving to the passenger door.

"Move your asses. We need to find a flushable toilet before I die of a bladder infection."

Sharing a glance with Lindsay that acknowledged both Addie's flair for the dramatic, and the futility of trying to send her home, we moved back toward the front of the car and programmed the nearest gas station into the navigation system.

Lucky for Addie's bladder, the nearest gas station was only five miles down the road, and we didn't need to divert to get to it. We managed to cover the distance with minimal complaints from the back seat, and before we knew it, she was sprinting for the gas station clerk for a restroom key.

I leaned my head on the steering wheel and groaned. What

was that kid thinking? She could've been in there for hours. Or worse, what if we'd been in an accident with no idea she was in there? Damn kid was gonna send me to an early grave way before Spells Hollow or those biker idiots got the chance.

"Is it illegal for us to abandon a teenager at a gas station?" I muttered against the wheel.

Lindsay patted me on the shoulder as he thought for a moment, "Technically, she's not ours to abandon. But depending on how you look at it, we might be kidnappers now. So... maybe? Definitely frowned upon."

"Shit. Fine. I'm gonna get us some gas while we're here."

I huffed and dragged myself out of the car while Lindsay headed inside, probably to top-up our snack stash now that we had a third mouth to feed.

As I filled up the tank, goosebumps prickled along my arms and the clouds darkened overhead. Perfect. Rain was just what this day needed. I glanced inside the building and spotted Lindsay strolling down an aisle, but where was... Aha! Addie's little blonde head bounced up to the register.

Maybe I was worrying for nothing. After all, there was a good chance this whole "Epic Road Trip of Destiny" would end up being a dud. I've been hit in the head a lot over the years, so who knows if it was real? Besides, we could totally keep Addie safe for a day or two. The home probably wouldn't even notice she's gone with how much time she usually spent with us.

We're gonna be fine, I reassured myself. *Addie's a good kid. We'll keep her close, away from danger, and out of tr—who the hell is she talking to now?*

I grabbed my hoodie from the back seat, pulling it on as I sprinted over to the store. My mother-hen instincts were fully in command of my brain as I skidded inside and put myself between Addie and the tall, blonde stranger she was eagerly chatting to.

"Hey, kiddo. Did you make it to the toilet in time, or do you need me to dig out your emergency panties?" I asked her, grinning at the opportunity to play the embarrassing guardian.

If looks could kill, I'd be stuck communicating through a Ouija board for the rest of time.

"You think you're funny, but you're not," she said before pushing past me and smiling at the guy I was supposed to be saving her from.

"Haven't you heard of stranger danger, kid?" I huffed and made a grab for her arm.

Evading me like the little shit she was, she took the guy's arm and dragged him toward the front of the store.

"He's not a stranger anymore. His name is Kylen, and he's heading the same way as us. I said that you'd give him a lift."

This time, I grabbed her arm with perfect accuracy, pulling her back a few steps as my thoughts buffered. "You did what now?"

"It's called being a good salvager—"

"Samaritan," I corrected her.

"Whatever." Addie folded her arms across her chest, avoiding my gaze. "I just think we should help him out."

To his credit, Kylen looked as awkward as I was furious. His eyes were constantly moving, flicking around at anything but me and Addie, while he gently scratched the light scruff on his jaw. His clothes were well-worn—cargo pants with a casual henley shirt, muddied hiking boots, and a light rain jacket—and I wondered how long he'd been on the road. He seemed like the woodsy-type, ready to camp out wherever he was comfortable.

"Hey, uh..." Kylen stepped towards me, an awkward smile twitching at his lips while he twisted his hands together. "You really don't have to give me a ride. I get that she was just being nice. I don't actually expect you to—"

Addie spun towards him in a blonde flurry. "I'm not 'just being nice'. It totally makes sense for you to come with us, or else you'll be walking all freakin' day!"

I couldn't take it anymore. With a quick shout to Lindsay to pay for the gas, I grabbed Addie's shoulders and steered her out into the rain, calling back to Kylen, "Excuse us a minute!"

As I tugged Addie's squirming body alongside the building, we ducked into a small alcove by a large dumpster where the rain wouldn't drench us as badly. Weird, it had started as a clear day.

"What the hell, Harlow?" Addie whined, pulling her hood over her hair.

"Oh, nuh-uh, kiddo. That's my question. What the hell is going on with you?" I asked, trying my damnedest to keep my voice level. The last thing I needed was someone overhearing, getting in the middle of this, and finding out Addie was technically missing. "First, you stowed away, and now you're inviting some rando to tag along? Addie, this trip isn't a joke."

"I know that, but you wouldn't have brought me otherwise, and you need me with you," Addie pleaded, her face serious. "Come on, you always tell me to trust my gut. I've got a good feeling about him, Harlow."

"You've had good feelings about farts. That doesn't mean you should invite them on a magical road trip!"

"Oh, I forgot to mention"—her eyes lit up as she completely ignored the point I was making—"Kylen's a witch! So it's already easier because you won't have to hide the sparky-sparky-zap-zaps."

My jaw dropped. This fucking kid.

"How did you already find out he was a witch? You were talking for like two seconds. Was your opening line, 'Hey, did you know supernaturals are real? Oh, you do! Which one are you?'"

A loud rumble in the parking lot pulled me from my rant, and my stomach dropped as I saw the source of the noise. I quickly pulled Addie down to crouch behind the dumpster, holding a finger to my lips.

Relieved at her compliance, I extended the finger, wordlessly asking for just a moment, and twisted around for another look to confirm my suspicions. The Grim Hearts MC's logo gleamed white on a large biker's leather jacket.

"What's going on?" Addie whispered. "You're acting really weird..."

"Listen to me, Addie." I held her shoulders, forcing her to look me in the eyes, and hoping she'd understand how serious I was. "I don't care what your gut tells you, but the guy on the bike is bad news. Now, I need you to go back inside, grab Lindsay and your friend, and get to the car."

Addie's eyes lit up. "We're bringing Kylen?"

I nodded. "No time to fight about it. If he wants a ride, then fine. I just want us all out of here safely. Can you go get them?"

"Yeah, no problem. What are you gonna do?"

Peeking around the dumpster, I spotted my least favorite psycho standing next to his bike, completely unbothered by the rain pouring around him. He stretched his leather-clad arms across his chest one after the other, then above his head as he leaned backwards. Damn, he really was in good shape.

Bad Harlow. Again with the ogling.

"I'm the one he's looking for, so I'll circle around the back to avoid him. Tell Lindsay to be ready to floor it as soon as I make it to you guys, okay?"

"Got it. See you in a minute." She turned to head back inside before spinning back to face me. "Oh, and, Harlow?"

"Yeah, kiddo?"

Addie bounced on her heels, her lips twitching as she

suppressed a mischievous grin, "When you see that I'm right about Kylen, can I adopt the dog?"

"I'm letting you bring an adult man. We can talk about the dog later."

I shooed her off and waited, crouched behind the dumpster, until I heard the faint *ding-a-ling* of the bell above the door.

Good, she's in.

In the gas station parking lot, my stalker tuged off his leather gloves with his teeth as he stomped past our car towards the store. And me.

I moved quickly, grateful for the pitter-pattering of rain against the dumpster to cover the sound of my boots as I rounded the corner to the back of the building. Staying low to avoid the windows, I shuffled between the wall and nearby trees, making it about halfway down before the doorbell rang out again.

Please, gods, let that be Addie leaving with the guys.

Too anxious about the situation to trust my luck, I peeked over the window frame and muttered a curse. Lindsay was still at the register with Addie and Kylen next to him. That meant the bell was... Shit!

I ducked out of sight just as I spotted a figure in a familiar leather jacket farther down the aisle, facing the windows I hid beneath. Wonderful. A chill ran down my shoulders as the rain soaked through my hoodie, but I did my best to ignore it. I just needed to keep moving, nice and slow.

Despite the barrier of brick and glass that separated us, I was painfully aware of the biker's presence. My heart pounded until I felt like I was choking on my own pulse. Taking a deep breath, I pushed myself to take another step, then another, and another, until I edged around the corner to a blessed full brick wall.

The doorbell rang again, and I breathed a sigh of relief as Addie's shrill voice urged Lindsay to "hurry the fuck up." Finally, we were nearly out.

I waited against the wall until I heard our car sputter to life, and then no force in the world could have stopped me. Keeping my hood up to hide my face, I sprinted to the car and dove into the open back door, my face landing on a pair of legs.

"Drive, Lindsay!" Addie shouted, and with a screech of tires, we were off.

Sitting up, I pulled the door shut as we swerved onto the road and took a deep breath.

"Nice one, Addie. I don't think he saw me." I cast a grin to my right, expecting to find my young apprentice.

Instead, the thighs my face had been pressed into belonged to the newest member of our chaotic troupe.

Addie threw me a cheeky grin from the front passenger seat, and I barely resisted giving myself a face-palm.

Welcome to the Epic Road Trip of Destiny, Kylen.

5

Kylen

"So... anyone wanna tell me what that was about?" I asked, shifting under the discomfort of the anxious energy buzzing through the car.

It seemed that, of everyone here, I was the least worried about the turn events had taken in the last thirty minutes, and I'd just been kidnapped.

Okay, so maybe *kidnapped* was an overstatement.

I had already accepted a ride before I was thrown in the car, after all. It had just been far more hurried than expected. One moment I'd been fielding questions from the little dud witch in front of me, and the next I was hustled into the back of the car like we were dodging paparazzi in the middle of LA.

I eyed the profile of the guy in the driver's seat. He could totally be a celebrity. His smooth, dark skin was expertly highlighted and powdered, and his eyelids shone with golden shadow framed with a dramatic dark wing of eyeliner. He was beautiful, and I could see him walking the carpet at the Met Gala. If I had any sense of self-preservation, I would be insanely attracted to him. Instead...

I slid my gaze toward the scowling bombshell to my left. Her arm stretched across the back of the seat, her fidgeting fingers brushing my shoulder as she shifted to check the road behind us at regular intervals. I wanted to ask her to sit down and buckle her seatbelt because the way she was half kneeling had images of blood and broken bones screaming through my head. Was a car accident likely? No. Was it worth the risk? Definitely not.

"Can you buckle up, please? Driving is dangerous in inclement weather, and the risk of a wreck increases exponentially with the deterioration of conditions."

She gave me an odd look, but thankfully reached for the belt and fastened it across her chest. An improvement, even if it wasn't what I'd hoped.

A low-level buzz vibrated in the air, an energy that made me twitch with the need to move. To do something. It increased with every unintentional brush of her fingers, and I felt a warmth building low in my gut. Cutting another look at my seatmate, I froze as realization dawned on me.

She was the source of the anxious feeling. And while most of it could be attributed to her behavior verging on paranoia, I knew some of it was something else. A knowing. We were meant to meet.

The fates were at play here.

"So..." I said, trying to catch her eye. She glared intently out the back window before finally sitting in her seat properly with a grunt.

"Addie tells me you're on a quest? That sounds exciting."

"Addie needs to keep her mouth shut."

I cringed, glancing toward the seat in front of me where the poor girl's shoulders were curled up to her ears. Harlow followed my gaze and sighed.

"It's fine. Yeah, we're on a full-on vision quest—"

"Epic Road Trip of Destiny," Lindsay crowed from the driver's seat.

Harlow rolled her eyes and pointed at the guy. "Yeah. That. Apparently, Spells Hollow is the place to be these days. Why are you going?"

I perked up, always happy to talk about my research.

"I'm a botanist. I've been searching for a rare plant for years. Actually, my mom first started the research, and I took it over when I finished my degree. The plant is supposed to have sedative properties that will revolutionize the way we practice medicine on supernatural beings, and I'm determined to find it. Do you know how many shifters have broken bones set poorly and then have trouble with their shift because of the speed of their healing? It's the same reason they can't be operated on. Their body absorbs the anesthetic too quickly for surgeons to operate. I learned that the local fauna in Spells Hollow is unique because of the town's history, so I'm hopeful this might be the place to find it."

"That sounds interesting."

I watched Harlow steadily for a moment, looking for the telltale signs of boredom, but while she wasn't as enthusiastic about the discussion as I was, she also wasn't already looking for the exit.

"So it's kinda like a family thing? Does your mom still help you with research?"

I flinched. The truth was, I hadn't had a mom for a long time now.

"My parents aren't around anymore. They died in a car accident when I was—"

"Dog!" Addie screeched, throwing her arm to point out Lindsay's window. The car swerved wildly before settling back on course. My heart leaped into my throat, and I briefly wondered if literally shitting myself in their car would be a stretch of this new friendship.

With a slow, deep breath, I encouraged my fingers to

release the death grip I had on the seat below me as the car straightened out. Shit. That was close.

"Jesus, fuck, Addie!" Lindsay growled, batting her hand away from his face.

"Did you see it? I swear, it was the same dog. He's following us!"

I glanced out the window. Rain streaked along the glass, and beyond it was a gray landscape where nothing appeared to move. "I don't see anything."

"He was there, I swear."

Harlow sighed and turned back to me. "Sorry. That was kind of shitty timing, considering what we were talking about."

"It's fine." I shrugged.

"So tell me more about botany."

We settled into an easy conversation, and it was less one sided than I feared. Harlow knew more about plants than I would have suspected, even if she did claim it was only things she remembered from high school. The way Lindsay snorted made me think it wasn't something she learned in science class. As the weather outside devolved into a howling, soggy mess of a day, I got to know the people I was traveling with.

Harlow chuckled. "So then Lindsay gets this bright idea to go under the fence with all the warning signs."

"They were more of a suggestion than a direction," he cuts in, his dark eyes gleaming with humor in the rearview mirror.

"And he was shocked when—"

Harlow cut off as the car lurched hard and fishtailed before Lindsay brought it back under control.

"Shit!"

"What was—"

A vaguely familiar motorbike pulled up to the driver's side window. The rider lifted his leg and kicked at the door. Harlow cursed, Addie screamed, and the seconds seemed to slow as a scene straight out of my nightmares played again. Lindsay tried to speed up and lose him, steering wide to avoid hurting the guy, but the wheels lost traction on the wet road, and the car went into a spin.

Gripping the seat with aching fingers, I saw it all play out. Broken glass. Blood. Silence. I couldn't handle going through it again. My chest heaved as images of little Addie covered in blood assaulted me. I'd just met her. I couldn't lose her already. I'd lost so much.

A face slowly registered in front of me. Resolving into two bright eyes, a delicate nose, and lips that looked tasty enough to kiss.

"You with us, big guy?" Harlow asked, squeezing my shoulder.

I blinked away the images in my mind's eye and looked around. The car had come to a stop facing a grassy field, completely undamaged and up the right way. I glanced around the interior and found everyone in the same shape they had been moments ago.

"I guess I overreacted a bit, huh?" I asked, rubbing the back of my neck with a self-conscious chuckle.

"Not at all. But now I know you're okay; I have some business to attend to." Harlow gave my shoulder one last reassuring squeeze and pushed out of the car to confront the asshole who had almost killed us.

"Isn't that the guy from the gas station?" I asked as Addie wriggled into the backseat to get a better view of the road.

"Yup. He's why we had to leave real quick. This is going to be so cool."

"Cool isn't the word I'd use," Lindsay grumbled, climbing through after her. "Someone crack open the window so we can hear better."

Outside, wind whipped at Harlow's hair as she stalked toward the asshole in black leather who leaned casually against his bike like he wasn't asking to be struck by lightning with all that metal under his butt.

"You can come after me; I don't give a shit. But you never threaten my family," she shouted over the howling gale.

The guy reached up and slowly drew off his helmet, turning to rest it on the seat of his bike. A now familiar buzzing streaked through my chest, and I cursed at the implication. Why was I always attracted to the dangerous ones? Dammit. Luckily, it seemed like I wasn't alone this time.

"Damn. If I wasn't so pissed about him threatening Harls, I'd take him for a ride. I swear I could change him."

I snorted at the earnest look on Lindsay's face.

"Unless you're going for a whole star-crossed lovers vibe, I don't think you and him are in the cards, my friend."

His shoulders slumped for a moment before he straightened with a wicked grin on his face. "Oh well. It'll be just as fun to see her hand him his ass."

I grunted in agreement and turned my attention back to the confrontation outside.

"I'll give you a choice. You can come with me, or I can kill you and leave you on the road."

"Why does he have to sound sexy when he's threatening the life of my bestie?" Lindsay moaned.

Addie elbowed him. "Ssh, I can't hear."

"I choose option C," Harlow growled, lifting her fingers to show—Was that electricity dancing over the tips?

"I've already seen your party trick. You're going to need a lot more than that." He raised his arms, and the rain intensified, the winds whipping at the water until it began to swirl in a controlled funnel, like a mini tornado.

"Shit. The storm is his," I breathed. Glancing at the two

beside me, I found matching smug grins on their faces. "What? What don't I know?"

"Just watch." Lindsay nodded toward the rear window. The biker had created a dense funnel of water that looked ready to crash into Harlow any minute.

"Come with me now or die."

Harlow threw her head back and laughed. The sound was slightly hysterical, but still filled me with warmth as she reached her hand toward the wall of water. Lightning arced from her fingertips, racing through the water and knocking the biker backwards over his bike.

In an instant, the rain stopped, and Harlow cursed as the water crashed down over her. Running her hands over her face, she stepped around the bike and crouched over the twitching form of the biker.

"I bet she's saying something cool, like *I told you I chose option C*," Addie whispered as we all watched in awe.

Harlow straightened and strode toward where we all huddled in the backseat.

"Should I have made popcorn for you?" she snarked, ruining the attitude with the affectionate smile she sent to the two beside me.

"That would have been great. Why didn't you think of it earlier?" Lindsay asked, opening the back door so we could all pile out. He headed straight toward the trunk and pulled out a towel. "Here. Do your best."

Harlow accepted the offering with a grunt.

"I think we need to take him with us. Can you guys move the bags to the backseat?"

I wasn't about to argue with the woman who'd just dropped someone with lightning, but I was curious if they were in the habit of kidnapping people. Or maybe it was just a kidnapping kind of day. Either way, now the weather had cleared, it took a relatively short amount of time to move the bags to the backseat and the unconscious man into the trunk.

Once everything was situated, Lindsay looked up the nearest motel, and we made a plan to meet there. Harlow slipped into the driver's seat and Addie called shotgun, so I squeezed in with the luggage as Lindsay mounted our new friend's bike.

"See you soon." He saluted and took off with a roar as we followed to find somewhere to dry off and get ready for an interrogation.

How the hell had my life changed so much in a matter of hours?

Harlow

THE SUN HAD JUST BEGUN to sink below the top of the tree line by the time we arrived at the Roadside motel. Spells Hollow was only a few more miles down the road, and the urge to continue on rode me hard, but with the delays we'd dealt with, it would be dark by the time we arrived. It was better to take the time to figure out who this biker was, rest, and start fresh tomorrow.

The motel was a sickly yellow color. Its walls looked thin as cardboard with wallpaper straight out of the seventies. Groovy. It looked like the setting for every road trip serial killer mystery ever written.

Spoiler alert, it was always the creepy owner.

"I can't believe this motel doesn't have a pool," Addie whined from where she'd flopped face down across the floral bedspread.

"We're lucky this place had adjoining twin rooms, let alone a damn pool." I huffed as I pulled a change of clothes from my duffel with shaking fingers.

While my explosion of energy on the highway had left me with some serious pep in my step, I was also soaked through and cold. It was just lucky Lindsay had taken the bike, or his splash back jokes would've been relentless on the ride here.

Despite the Camry's heaters running full blast, the cold had settled into my bones. A hot shower and cup of cocoa were in my immediate future. I couldn't fucking wait to feel my toes again.

"You okay staying here a few minutes?" I asked her.

Without lifting her head, she flashed a thumbs up and snuggled up to a pillow. At least she couldn't cause trouble if she was taking a nap.

After double checking the room's locks, I left a trail of wet clothes to the bathroom and hopped in the shower. The water wasn't anywhere near as hot as I'd like it, but it was enough to get my joints moving again. Once dressed in a pair of sweats and a loose tank top usually reserved for sleeping, I finally felt more like myself. I was squeaky-clean, and the build-up of excess magic I usually had bubbling inside me was gone. If it weren't for the biker gang trying to kill me, I could skip to Spells Hollow.

A knock came at the motel room door as I was towel drying my hair. I stepped out of the bathroom in a cloud of steam as Addie hauled herself to the door to admit Lindsay.

"Lemme tell you, I think I understand bikers now," he announced. "Like, I could get used to having something that powerful between my thighs."

Addie made a gagging noise as she jumped back on the bed she'd claimed. "Ew. Please, say less before I have to surgically remove my ears."

"You spoil all my fun." Lindsay pouted at her before turning to me. "I've chained the bike to a tree at the back of the building."

"Thanks. Hopefully, our 'drunk buddy' won't get loose." I said, chuckling at the memory of Lindsay and Kylen dragging his unconscious body inside past the motel owner.

"Kylen's secured him. We got a name from his ID, by the

way: Bruin. Not sure if it's a first name, surname, or just one word like Cher, but it's something."

"How's he doing in there?" I nodded to the adjoining room.

"He's awake, twitchy, and raging something fierce. Oh, and *fucking* pretty." Lindsay fanned himself with one hand. "If I wasn't still obsessing over what Kedron said to me, I'd be all over him."

"Still not sure where you stand?"

"Nope." He sighed dramatically, taking a seat on the bed next to Addie. "He's wriggled his way from my pants to my heart."

"Like a blood clot of emotion," Addie said, wrapping her arms around his waist. "Do you think we could talk about this over waffles?"

Lindsay hugged her back with a grin. "Fuck yes, that sounds so good right now. I think I saw a diner over the road, next to the gas station."

"I'll catch up to you guys later," I said, glaring at the wall as though I could burn the man next door with my mind. "It's about time I had a chat with our pretty little psycho."

***

I headed through the door linking our two rooms once Lindsay and Addie had left. We had agreed to only keep it locked from our side to keep Addie safe if Bruin got out. It also meant we could quickly get to Kylen in the same scenario.

"How's my favorite asshole doing?" I asked cheerily.

His response was a dangerous scowl, along with a middle finger, despite his bound hands.

His whole body was restrained. Ropes wrapped around his torso, thighs, ankles, and almost seemed to writhe around parts of his body. Curious, I looked closer and... were those vines?

"Botany's more useful than people give it credit for." Kylen flashed a boyish smile from the armchair in the corner. His long legs dangled over one side, and he'd put on a pair of round-framed glasses since we'd split into our rooms. Noticing my stare, he adjusted them on his nose. "I prefer them over contacts."

"They suit you." I smiled, surprised by how comforting I found his presence. He radiated a calm energy that soothed the tension in the room.

"If you're gonna stand there flirting like high schoolers, can you knock me out again first?" Bruin snarled from the bed.

Unlike our other guest.

"Ooh, someone's a grouchosaurus rex," I teased.

Bruin's muscles flexed under the vine's grip, unable to move an inch. "Gee, I wonder why."

As if to prove his point, the vines wiggled around him, splitting off in places and exploring under the hem of his black t-shirt.

"Hey! Watch where those vines are going!" he snapped, squirming on the bed until they retreated to their original position.

"Sorry about that." Kylen chuckled. "They have a mind of their own sometimes, but they're harmless, I swear."

Bruin raised both eyebrows. "Oh, you're a kinky little twink, aren't ya?"

Kylen's eyes widened before he looked at me, pointing at himself and mouthing the question, "Twink?"

Turning back to the furious biker, I pursed my lips and bit back the same shit-eating grin Addie liked to use on me. "Look, I get it. That fight on the highway was super embarrassing for you. I almost feel bad about it, but then I remember that incident with the knife and your friends in the alley..."

Swaying from one foot to the other, I mentally weighed the

two situations and came up about even. Not a drop of guilt. "You had it coming, and you underestimated me."

"A mistake I won't make twice," he promised.

The determined look in his eyes left me with no doubt he meant it. I almost wanted to let him go so I could take him on again. Could be fun.

Pushing down the impulsive thoughts, I took a seat on the bed next to him, patting the vines wrapped around his thighs with a condescending smile.

"Oh!" I gasped as the vine pulsed beneath my hand. A thin stem sprouted between my fingers and grew into a tiny white bloom. "How cute. I guess they like me."

"Well, that makes one of us," he deadpanned.

"That's too bad." I plucked the small flower and gently placed it in the longer, mussed strands at the top of his hair. "Aw, how pretty!"

Bruin's jaw ticked.

"Now, I'm more than happy to get all these vines off you and watch you ride off into the sunset on that bike of yours. But I'm gonna need you to agree to, y'know..." I waved a hand in the air, searching for the right words. "Leave me the fuck alone."

"And why the hell would I do that?"

"Fair question. Let's say, because I could kill you right now. Probably wouldn't be the first murder in one of these rooms."

Bruin's laugh cracked across the space between us. "Hah! That's an empty threat if I ever heard one. You're a cunt, not a killer, sweetheart."

Hm. Couldn't deny that.

"So let me tell you what's actually going to happen," he continued. "You may not be a killer, but I am. And you fucked with my club, so you're gonna pay for it. I don't care how you die, but the prez wants it done. That means a fucking good payout for me. Tell me, do you know how long someone can stay alive if they have water? I can wait you out, bitch, but you won't be escaping me. Whether I kill you back at the club, or here on the road, Prez is gonna love seeing your drowned corpse."

Bruin hissed as the vines visibly tightened at his words. Rather than apologizing, he turned a dark grin on Kylen. "Oh, they didn't like that at all. How interesting."

The nature witch waved a hand at the vines, and they relaxed their grip, though they still looked uncomfortably tight. He flashed a concerned look at me, which I returned with a nod. Things were fine. I could handle his threats.

"Sadly, none of that's gonna work for me." I took a deep breath, readying myself to explain this crappy situation I'd been thrown into that made the MC look like the smallest, most adorable potatoes by comparison. Guess it would be news to Kylen, too. "You see, I'm on this blood-moon-vision-quest-thing. Crazy big deal, or so I'm told. And I really don't have the time or the patience to deal with a bunch of butthurt biker egos before finding out if I'm gonna live to see next month."

Silence filled the room as I struggled to unclench my jaw. Did I really believe that my life could be in danger from this quest?

Your time is as short as your temper.

I'd be an idiot not to see that comparison didn't work in my favor.

Kylen gave my shoulder a reassuring squeeze. I hadn't even heard him move over to me, but his presence helped me steel my spine.

"So let's make a deal," I offered, meeting Bruin's surprised gaze. "You give me the time to deal with this quest. A few days to see what's what and potentially save my own life. Then, once that's done, I'll go with you willingly."

Bruin's eyes narrowed, searching for the catch in my offer.

I pressed on. "Think about it. You were ready to kill me yourself, so I might save you the trouble. And on the off-chance I save myself, you get to bring me back, brownie points and whatever payout to you, and we'll see how your boy band fares against me a second time."

A laugh bubbled out of him, half genuine and half mocking. "Fuck it! You're dead either way, aren't you?"

"Thought you weren't going to underestimate me again?"

"True. Tell you what, I'll take your deal on one condition. You let me follow you on your little vision quest."

"Don't trust me not to run away?"

His grin widened. "That, and I want a front-row seat to your death."

***

The fucking nerve of that asshole.

Gravel crunched under my boots as I stomped from the motel to the diner. Despite the agreement to let Bruin tag along and watch my potential death, I wasn't ready for Kylen to release him from the vines in case he tried something during the night. This left me playing delivery girl for the two of them.

Forget blood moon vision quests; my latest mission was getting takeout. Hopefully, there wasn't as much risk of death with this quest.

A chilled breeze swept around me, and I shivered, regretting not grabbing a sweater before I left. There was something in the air around here that didn't sit right with me. As I crossed the small dirt road separating the motel from the diner and gas station, I felt the same pull from the vision. We were close to Spells Hollow.

Pulling up the map on my phone and comparing it with the

directions from Reddit, I could see I was right. The town was just over five miles down that road. A short drive, or a decent woodland hike for a city girl like me.

As I walked past the woods, my gaze fixed on my phone, a warm wall of muscle suddenly blocked my path and jolted me out of my thoughts, making me drop my phone in surprise. At least I didn't zap it, I guess.

"Ah! Oh, shit, sorry!" I scrambled on the ground for my phone. I'd only just finished paying it off a few weeks ago, and I was determined to get every penny's worth now.

A deep grunt distracted me from my phone retrieval as the man crouched in front of me and easily palmed the elusive device.

"If you're not careful with your things, they'll break," a deep voice, smooth as melted chocolate, said. Despite the condescending tone, my limbs turned to Jell-O.

He offered me my phone in a large, tanned hand and straightened.

I finally looked up at him, and up... and up... Wow, this guy made me feel dainty. He could throw me over his shoulder, and I'd have to stretch to slap his ass.

"G'night." The speed of his departure would've been offensive if it hadn't given me a view that confirmed my suspicion—his ass was totally slap-able.

As I stepped away, mentally mourning the loss of "dat ass"—as my mind had already dubbed it—something tapped against my boot.

Huh. I haven't seen a pair of these for ages.

"Hey! Wait up!" I shouted, jogging after him back towards the motel. He moved quickly, but I caught him just before he reached the building. "You dropped these. Lucky I didn't step on them."

His mahogany eyes narrowed at the pair of wired earphones I held out to him.

"I mean, I'm guessing they're yours," I started babbling. "I haven't seen someone use these outside of a last resort for years. Even Addie got a Bluetooth headset for her birthday a few years back."

I bit the inside of my cheek, begging myself to stop verbally digging my grave.

"They're mine," he growled, snatching them from my hand. His scowl was dark but still kinda cute. I hated that he could be rude and attractive all at once. That right there was pretty privilege.

"My bad. Should've been looking where I was going, but it's been a long-ass day." I glanced at the diner, then back to the man. "Just need to get some food in me and then I can crash for the night."

His gaze raked over me, and not in a fun way. This would have been a great time for my mouth to stop with all the words, but there was something about him that made me want him to notice me. Either that, or I was way more tired than I thought, and my verbal filter had gone on vacation.

"Well, I should let you go." I forced an awkward smile, backing away slowly. "Sorry, again."

He nodded once, his auburn curls bouncing just above his shoulders, before he unlocked the motel room next to ours.

The door clicked shut behind him, and I strolled toward the diner as the conversation replayed in my head. Damn, his voice really did something to my bones. Now that was a man I should go after. But no, the man I've been closest to lately was trying to kill me. Typical.

Although Kylen seemed like a good guy. He definitely rolled with the punches of the day, no denying that.

Ugh, I shouldn't be worrying about this crap. I need food and a bed, that's it. Calm down, vagina. We're on a quest to a spooky old town, not a booty call.

By the time I picked up a few burger meals, my exhaustion had seriously caught up with me. I took a moment to myself in the motel parking lot, leaning against the Camry while Lindsay and Addie bounded out to relieve me of the food and disappeared back inside.

Hopefully, we'd at least get some sleep before we finally got to Spells Hollow tomorrow. That was all I could wish for at that moment. But judging by Addie's cackling laughter echoing through the paper-thin walls, I doubted it. She was so excited to be out of the city, despite the reason we were here.

Fuck, I don't want her to watch me die.

Hendrix

After a sleepless night, thanks to my inconsiderate neighbors, I was in a foul mood as I packed my bags to continue my journey. The bumping and thumping of several people moving around set my teeth on edge. Why was the world full of neanderthal lesser beings who didn't understand the concept of courtesy? They were in a motel. People could be trying to sleep, dammit. The slamming of their door thundered through my room, and I grimaced, partially relieved they were finally out, but also more mad than ever that they couldn't close a goddamn door quietly.

I wandered toward the window, pulling the curtain out of the way just enough to glimpse the dark-haired woman I'd spoken to the day before. She was as crass as the rest of her party, but also... intriguing?

With a huff, I released the curtain and returned to my luggage. Today was the day. I could feel it. Treasure was close, and nothing would stand in the way of me making it mine. My spine itched with the urge to release my wings and take to the skies. To feel the wind in my mane and clouds chilling my paws. Soon.

From what I'd read, Spells Hollow was deserted. Some silly

tale of ghosts and curses kept the dullard masses at bay, which meant no one would be around to notice an 850-pound gryphon flying around. Not that I personally cared about the exposure, but my clan had been hunted in years gone by, and I didn't want to deal with the headache it would all bring about. It would divert me from my true calling: treasure hunting.

Dragons may have been well known in pop culture for hoarding treasure, but my kind could sense it. We were far superior to those flying lizards in every way. Case in point: because they couldn't keep their mouths shut about their hoard, plus the whole stealing women thing, they had barely survived the centuries of genocide humans brought down upon them.

A vibration started in my chest as the roar of an engine outside announced the motel was finally free of my raucous neighbors.

"Not a minute too soon," I muttered, checking the room for anything out of place.

The bed was neatly made after my terrible night's sleep, nothing on the floor beneath it. The wet towel was in the tub, as per the sign posted in the bathroom. My toothbrush and toothpaste were tucked in a plastic bag in my backpack, with my dirty laundry in a separate bag in the back pocket. I'd meant to launder it the night before, but that woman and her crew had thrown me out of routine.

I scratched my chest, glancing at the remote controls for the television to ensure they were straight, before hiking the bag over my shoulder and retrieving my key card from the small table under the window.

Right before I stepped out the door, I retrieved my iPod from the side pocket of my bag and threaded the headphone wire through the front of my shirt. Tucking the buds into my ears, I hit play and felt my shoulders drop as Sam Sparro filtered into my head, singing "Black and Gold". My cousin had tried unsuccessfully to upgrade my music choices and the device I listened to them on, but there was something material about having the system connected. To know I can pull the plug if I need to use the headphones as a garotte at a moment's notice. You couldn't do that with a Bluetooth headset. Even throwing it at someone wouldn't slow them down.

Stepping outside, I gently pulled the door closed, because I wasn't a heathen, and paused at the empty parking spot.

They're gone.

"Good."

Trudging across the parking lot, I braced myself to deal with the unwashed masses for a greasy breakfast.

"How you doin', honey?"

Barely a step into the diner, and I'd already drawn unwanted attention. The waitress smiled cheerily, rosy cheeks spread wide to show perfect white teeth. Despite the warmth of her expression, ice slid down my spine as she waved me toward an empty booth. Popping out an earbud, I nodded in greeting and moved quickly past her.

"Our special today is pumpkin pie with walnut cream. Can I get you a coffee?"

"Thanks," I muttered, eyeing the cherry pie on display by the register. Was she messing with me?

The scent of old grease and sugary sweet perfume hung in her wake as she moved around the deserted diner, retrieving my coffee and a laminated menu for me to peruse. I sighed, leaning back in my seat and looking out the window toward the motel. Maybe I should have booked another night so I could be sufficiently rested before I continued on my hunt. Spells Hollow could be dangerous according to what I could find on the place in the urban explorer chat rooms. People go in and never return. I wasn't just *people*, but with the way gravity pulled at my bones after last night, I needed to be sure I had my wits about me before venturing into the unknown.

A tiny elderly woman in an obnoxiously gaudy leopard print top and pink pants emerged from the motel's reception area hauling a bucket and mop. Her lips moved at lightning speed as though cursing someone out. I thought of the neighbors I'd had the previous night. The reason my sleep had been so poor in the first place. Nope. Camping was definitely the better choice.

"Here you go, dear. Now, what can I get you to eat?" The waitress patted her perfectly styled hair and pulled a notepad from her apron.

"What's the camping like around here?" I asked, sipping my coffee and hiding a grimace as the stale sludge slid over my tongue.

"Best in the country. The farther into the woods you go, the better it gets. Some people never want to leave."

I grunted, wondering if I'd have to compete with other campers, but dismissed the thought quickly. This place was deserted and the only other travelers I'd seen were the neighbors from last night who had already left. I'd be fine. I placed an order for a full breakfast of eggs, bacon, and sausage on waffles and took the time to plan the next leg of my trip. My skin buzzed with the sense of treasure close by, and I knew this one would be life changing.

After wolfing down my meal, including the coffee—because caffeine was caffeine when I was tired enough to feel my pulse in my eyeballs—I paid and headed toward the motel parking lot where my 1967 Ford Eleanor 500GT sat waiting for me. I'd debated leaving her here and hiking in, but the itch under my skin leant an urgency to the hunt that would make the rough two-hour walk unbearable.

Turning over the ignition, I closed my eyes and felt the roar of the engine coming to life beneath my hands. Popping my earbud back in place, I pulled out of the parking space and turned toward the long road to Spells Hollow, humming to Spandau Ballet singing about *gold.* My favorite subject, and hopefully some of the treasure I'd find in the mysterious town ahead.

As the car bumped along the increasingly neglected road, my gut churned with a sense of unease. Chills skittered along my arms, making the hair stand on end. Magic. No wonder this town had such a reputation. Trying to shake off the effects, I rolled down my window and focused on steering around the potholes that threatened to destroy my car's suspension.

By the time I pulled up to the remains of a broken and rotted gate, I was done. I could practically feel the damage to the car's undercarriage, and I wasn't having it. Pulling the car up parallel with the fence, I killed the engine and rooted in the backseat for my car cover. The spot I'd chosen was relatively clear of trees, so there wouldn't be any damage from falling limbs, and once the cover was in place, the paintwork would also be safe. Not a foolproof plan, but definitely better than continuing to drive.

Once the car was locked tight and covered, I shouldered my backpack and made my way through the gate. A metallic crunch underfoot drew my attention to a small sheet of metal marked *KEEP OUT*. Magical wards, physical signs... this place grew more interesting by the second. Beyond the sign, tire tracks proved how ineffective both warnings had been to previous visitors. Curiosity won every time.

Taking a deep breath of fresh air, I decided to give in to my earlier impulse. I wouldn't walk the last mile into town. I would fly. It had been weeks since I was able to stretch my wings, and the promise of freedom was too much to resist. I dropped my bag in the dust and backed away a few steps, reaching deep to find the beast within. It cried in triumph, a loud keening sound as fur sprouted from my skin and my bones cracked with the change.

The first time I ever shifted, the pain had been blinding. Barely into puberty, I'd shifted long before I'd gotten my first erection. The intensity of the experience made me blackout, and when I'd woken in a body I couldn't control, I'd found a single gold coin on the pillow beside me.

Gryphons didn't buy into the tooth fairy myth. No Santa Claus or Easter Bunny, but our first shift was sacred, and it was marked by the gifting of our first piece of treasure.

Much like it had that first time, my sense of the proximity of treasure doubled as my wings expanded across my back. I dropped onto my paws and stretched back, enjoying the pull along my spine and through my shoulders. Thank whatever magic created gryphons that my clothes shifted with me, because I didn't have the space on my hunts for endless clothing changes. With a lazy flick of my tail, I scooped my backpack up with two claws.

It's time.

Rearing onto my hind legs, I beat my wings and screeched in joy as my paws left the ground. In a matter of seconds, I cleared the top of the trees and saw the land stretch out toward the sea below me. The wind whipped at my beak, ruffling my mane as I swooped toward the tree line and climbed up through the cloud cover a couple of times, enjoying the freedom of flight.

With the sharpened vision of my gryphon form, I caught movement in the woods. Bears, wolves, a white lone wolf that almost seemed to be watching me. They were as insignificant as the humans I'd left behind at the diner. Nothing mattered when I was chasing updrafts and tasting the cold moisture of low-hanging clouds. Nothing except...

My beak twitched, and I turned toward the cluster of buildings on the cliff's edge. Spells Hollow. Treasure.

Turning into a lazy downward spiral, I aimed for a clearing beside the river that ambled around the outskirts of town before cutting through the cliff side. I looked back toward the woods, considering heading deeper to find a good campsite for the night. Eh, the sun was nowhere near its zenith yet, and the call of treasure begged me to head toward town. Shaking out my mane, I took a deep breath and called to the man inside me, releasing the beast with a promise to fly again soon.

The scent of salt and seaweed danced in my nostrils as the onshore wind swept over me, invigorating me on my walk as I passed dilapidated buildings that would have housed working-class families in years gone by. Some were little more than rubble, collapsed chimneys, and rotten log cabins, but every now and then I would glimpse one whose frame had withstood the battering of the elements.

According to my research, it had been three hundred and fifty-odd years since Spells Hollow was a thriving community. Centuries since some event, lost to time, had caused the inhabitants to abandon the town. I could admit that the history buff in me was almost as interested in finding out what happened here as I was in the treasure that called to me like the sweetest siren song.

The earth crunched beneath my boot, and I glanced down, frowning at the dark line on the ground. Glancing left and right, I noticed it extended out on both sides. Behind me, the grass grew green and lush, the trees plentiful. Before me, there was only death. Dirt and shriveled stalks that may once have been plants littered the ground, and I wondered what could have caused such a marked distinction between the two. It was as though someone had burned and salted the earth. Like life had been leached from everything this side of the line.

Like a curse.

The soft murmur of voices reached me from the far side of the nearest house. This one appeared to be in far better repair than the ones I had passed earlier. Two stories high, it had not only maintained its walls, but most of its windows, too. Keeping hidden from whoever else had decided to explore the abandoned town, I moved closer to the house, noting there were several others that appeared to be arranged in a circle around the town square. I wished I'd taken the time to map out the town while I was airborne, but the novelty of flight had outweighed my curiosity about the town while I was up there. No chance of flying now, though. I had company.

Huffing in annoyance, I quietly circled the house, hoping to catch a glimpse of the interlopers and barely suppressed a curse. A familiar dark head and admittedly spectacular ass was climbing the stairs to the front door. Behind her, the noisy entourage from last night continued to bicker and jest.

Of all the abandoned towns in all the world, she had to walk into mine.

And if she was after my treasure, we were going to have a problem.

A low growl caught my attention. I swung around, coming face to face with the white wolf I'd spotted earlier; although now I was closer, I knew he wasn't just any white wolf. He was a raiju, a creature native to Japan, whose powers were linked to lightning.

"You're a long way from home, pup," I murmured.

His lip curled as the low growl came again. I could take him with my eyes closed, but something in the back of my mind cautioned that the animal could be useful. Holding my hands up, I took a careful step away from the house and turned my back on the stampede of feet entering it.

"Nothing to worry about. I'm not here for them."

The wolf chuffed, his hackles dropping as he moved forward and took a long inhale. His thick tail twitched a half wag before he turned and disappeared between the buildings.

Maybe I'd made a new friend.

Not that I needed one.

Harlow

"Are the vines still necessary?" Bruin asked, raising his bound hands with an irritation that continued to amuse me the longer it lasted.

We'd squished him between Kylen and me in the middle seat of the Camry, and I immediately missed those beautiful hours the day before when he'd been unconscious in the trunk. Good times.

"Yep. I don't trust you not to try something while we're driving. Now shush," I snapped back before leaning forward to flick Addie on the shoulder. "Hey, eyes front, kiddo! No conversations with the hostage allowed."

"Hostage? Really?" Bruin muttered.

Addie slumped in her seat, unusually grumpy despite being in her preferred shotgun position. Honestly, she was lucky we didn't leave her in the motel. If I thought she wouldn't hike through the woods to follow us, I would have.

She muttered something I couldn't hear, but it made Lindsay laugh from the driver's seat. "Aww, Addie's getting maddie," he teased, reaching over with one hand to ruffle her hair.

"Oh my *gawd*! You suck so hard!"

"Funnily enough, Kedron said the same thing to me last week." Lindsay winked at me in the rearview mirror, and I snorted.

Addie went quiet for a moment, processing his words. "Dude. Pull over, I gotta puke."

"Seconded," Bruin grunted.

"No need, prudes," Lindsay said, slowing the car to a stop as the woodland road opened up. "I think this is it."

Leaning out of the passenger window, an old, rotting gate loomed ahead of us. It was too modern to be the original town gate, but the metal was rusted and frail. "Everyone, stay here for a minute. Don't touch the car doors or anything made of metal."

I slid out of the car and gripped the remains of the gate tight with both hands. With a deep breath, I pushed out with my magic, like I would blow out a few too many candles. Electricity crackled across the metal, fizzling and sparking until the whole thing blew apart with a crash.

As the dust settled, I stepped over the threshold, hesitating for just a moment when my foot tapped a thin, metal KEEP OUT sign. Well, I'd never been one for doing what I was told.

"Welcome to Spells Hollow, I guess."

Lindsay drove us the final mile into town, finally pulling over between the tree line and a huge derelict building. We exited the car and slowly circled around the side of the structure. It was a lot bigger and more intricate than what I imagined an original colony house would look like. The wood was burnt, but still held together. Impressive, considering how long the town had supposedly been abandoned. But there was a lot we didn't know about this place.

As we reached the front and stared out at the town proper, it became obvious that this was more than a deserted settlement. All around us, buildings stood in various states of disrepair, where they weren't reduced to a pile of rubble, all the way up to a line on the ground that separated a perfectly preserved slice of history.

"Wait a minute." I crouched, brushing the point where charred earth met clean, healthy grass with my fingertips. "Lindsay, can you sense any spells along this line? Any illusions?"

The line was a literal scorch mark in the grass. From where we stood, it seemed to surround the interior of the town in a circle, but we'd need to keep walking to know for certain.

My bestie kneeled beside me, placing both hands along the strange line, and closed his eyes. I glanced around while he concentrated on working his magic and found Bruin leaning against the large building behind us, permanent scowl in place. Guess he was serious about not letting me out of his sight. Ugh, what a pain.

Speaking of pains... Addie was following Kylen like a duckling as he poked his head around a few buildings, keeping close for now. He didn't seem to mind her presence, though. In fact, he kept up a running monologue of each thing he studied so she could understand what they were doing. Maybe this would end up being a weird history field trip for her.

After a few minutes, Lindsay sat back on his heels with a sigh. "I know this town is supposed to be magical and shit, but dude, this town is magic. Like old-school-protection-spells kinda magic. It feels like they're just around the houses, which might explain the difference in the grass, but we should still be careful what we touch. Good news is I don't sense anything that would immediately hurt us. So that's a win."

I offered him a hand up. "I'll happily take 'not immediately hurt.'"

"It's a lovely change of pace for you." He chuckled, dusting off his knees and glancing around. "Where the hell do we start?"

Pursing my lips, I moved over the line into the preserved section of town, spinning on my toes for one step, two... As I landed the third step, I pointed in a random direction. "This way!"

"That's how you're making your decisions?" Bruin snarked as he followed close behind.

"Usually, no. But when you're on a magical vision quest—"

"Epic Road Trip of Destiny," Lindsay corrected.

"Epic Road Trip of Destiny." I nodded at Lindsay, who motioned for me to continue. "You need to let fate take the wheel now and then."

Just as I thought Bruin's eyes were going to roll back far enough for him to see the empty cavity where his brain should be, Addie shouted, "Hey! I'm gonna stay with Kylen and look for plants!"

Kylen flashed a thumbs up to approve the message, and after a moment of thought, I nodded. Now that we knew him a little more, he seemed safe enough for Addie to hang with while they looked around the town, especially if they were staying outside. She might actually learn a thing or two from him.

"Okay. But stay close and meet back here in two hours!"

We moved carefully around the town square, not approaching the gallows in the center. I wasn't ready to start off my exploration with something that deadly, so I started looking through the windows in a few of the surrounding businesses. Because obviously if I was going to watch someone die, I'd need retail therapy afterwards. Yikes.

Continuing in the direction fate had dictated for me, we ended up in front of a row of three large houses surrounded by gardens and wooden fences. The houses seemed to circle the town square, and I wondered if it was mirrored on the other side. I'd have to check later. As I stared up at the first house, my heartbeat accelerated, and warmth spread through my chest. It felt like... home? No, this was nuts. I'd never been here before, but the feeling of familiarity wouldn't stop nagging my brain.

Bruin appeared in my path, pulling me out of my thoughts as he snapped, "Are you just gonna stare at it, or are we going inside one of these creaking deathtraps?"

"Calm your murder-boner, psycho." I shouldered past him through the front gate, and the closer I got to the front door, the more it felt like I was going to barf up my own heart.

The doorknob was cool beneath my shaking hand, and I took a calming breath before gently turning—

"Did you hear that?" Bruin asked, his head whipped around as he pressed his back to the wall beside me, more cautious than earlier with his hands bound in Kylen's vines.

Neither Lindsay nor I moved for a moment, listening for whatever he had picked up on.

Bruin's eyes narrowed. "I swear I heard growling. Like a bear or a wolf."

"Or your stomach?" I quipped, finally opening the door to reveal a large foyer.

Thick, musty air filled my lungs as I stepped inside, my footsteps muffled by the russet patterned rugs covering most of the hardwood floors. A thick layer of dust covered the surfaces of wooden tables and cabinets along the wall leading to the dining room on my right. With a heavy pull, I opened the floor-length drapes, allowing sunlight to fill the space for the first time in centuries.

"Let's open a window in here," Lindsay muttered, fiddling with the locks before welcoming in an ocean breeze. "That should make it a bit easier to breathe."

Now that light filtered into the space, I could see that the table stretched through a room much longer than I thought it'd be. Whoever lived here was either very rich or very powerful. Picking up a plate from the edge of the table, I blew the dust off before shining it with the hem of my t-shirt. It was heavy, gleaming real silver in the sunlight.

"Well, at least no one's leaving here poor." Bruin smirked, opening a drawer to find matching silverware.

"Of course your first thought is to loot the place," I scolded him, though there was a thought at the back of my mind that we could really use the money. Hell, depending on how haunted this place was, maybe we could move in.

In the next room, toward the back of the house, I found a kitchen the size of our apartment. Holy shit, people could cook actual meals here, as a family, instead of fighting over a stovetop where only half the burners worked. Except for the dust, everything was in an amazing condition, clearly well cared for before it was abandoned. Which begged the question, who would leave a house like this?

We completed a circle of the ground floor, walking through a large sitting area with multiple couches and armchairs where the family must have gathered, and a conservatory with a view of the tragically overgrown garden. I made a mental note to show it to Kylen in case this family had grown his mysterious plant. It looked like a miniature jungle out there.

As we headed for the stairs, a whistling sound from below distracted me. Did this house have a basement? Smoothing my hands along the wooded wall under the stairs, I felt a cool breeze from between two planks of wood. "Hey, Lins! Gimme some light over here?"

He held up his phone, the flashlight shining on the side of the staircase, and I followed the gap to a spot big enough I could pull with my fingertips. With barely a hint of effort, a door swung open like it was welcoming me inside. That was far too easy.

"Do you see anything?" Lindsay asked.

I nodded. "Stairs. It looks like they might lead underground. Wanna take a look?"

"At the definitely-not-haunted secret tunnel? I think I'll try upstairs instead."

"Oh, boo. Come on, I've got a good feeling about this."

Lindsay held up his hands in surrender. "You do you. I'm more interested in what's on the second floor."

"Okay. Meet in an hour."

"*Ahem.*" Bruin held out his bound hands, looking more like a Victorian orphan boy than the biker threatening to murder me. "Come on, Sparky. I know you don't want me alone with your friend, and if we're going down there, I'm gonna need my hands to dig myself out when it collapses."

He had a point, sort of. At least if he was with me, I could keep an eye on him. Plus, I'd already beat him once.

"Do you seriously think you can trust him?" Lindsay asked, eyeing him.

I stifled a laugh as I carefully zapped the vines enough for them to release their captive. Didn't want them to accidentally constrict him instead and squeeze off his arms... or did I? Now there's a thought.

"Not even a little. But I know I could make lightning tap dance across his ass if he starts shit."

"At least I know you're thinking about my ass." Bruin winked at me, shaking off the last of the vines that had plagued him for the past day.

"I think you *are* an ass. Now, let's go."

Crouching to avoid the low ceiling, we headed down into the earth.

Harlow

"Those vines left sap all over my skin. Ugh, I'm all sticky, and now we're ignoring all the signs of an imminent cave-in and heading underground."

"Do you ever stop bitching?" I asked, whirling on Bruin and almost losing my balance on the uneven stairs.

His hand snapped out and gripped my upper arm, steadying me as I caught my footing. My skin prickled at the contact, and we both froze, stares fixed on his hand.

"Uh... thanks," I said, awkwardly twisting out of his grip before continuing my descent.

After a few moments, his footsteps echoed behind me.

"So what do you think is down here?" he asked as we hit the bottom of the stone stairs and faced off with a heavy wooden door.

"I don't know. That's why I'm down here."

I reached out and traced the jagged lines of metal worked into the face of the door. It looked like forked lightning crawling from the top of the door almost to the floor. I smiled at the image, thinking of my own ability and feeling a moment of kinship with whoever had crafted it.

"What are you smiling at? Let's get going so we can get back out in the fresh air. It's claustrophobic down here."

"Naww... Is someone scared of small spaces? Would you rather go back to being locked in the trunk?"

The flat look he sent me caused a chuckle to bubble out of my throat. It wasn't my fault he was fun to goad. When he refused to dignify my teasing with a response, I sighed and pushed the door open to reveal a long passage carved into the bedrock. There were metal sconces with large clear crystals set into the walls at head height, and as I stepped through the door, the crystals closest flared to life, casting a warm yellow light around the immediate area.

Bruin coughed, then sneezed, sending me a look through bloodshot eyes that clearly said he wasn't impressed. So it was a little dusty. There was a whole lot of history in this town and, just maybe, an answer to this pesky quest that my survival seemed to depend upon.

No pressure.

"You could have waited upstairs with the others, you know."

I hazarded a glance at my annoying sidekick and clenched my jaw at the wicked smirk on his face. Why did the guy trying to kill me have to be so damn good looking? It wasn't fair. From the scar through his thick, dark eyebrow to his tatted-up body, the man was made for sex. Maybe I'd go there if I could find a ball gag big enough to fit his annoying mouth.

"Did you get a good enough look?"

Shit. Rule number one: Don't get caught ogling the delicious bad guy.

Instead of answering, I chose a direction at random and moved farther into the catacombs. Crystals lit up as I approached, and behind us, I could see them fading back into darkness as they were no longer needed. Magic was so cool.

Small pockets had been carved into the walls, and while most were empty, some had small trinkets. A metal bowl, a horse carved from wood, each item was crafted with impressive skill considering the age of the town. Despite being made in a time before laser cutting and 3D printing, the detail was exquisite.

Around a slight curve in the tunnel, we came across another door. As I laid my hand on the aged wood, I got the sense I wasn't welcome. The feeling wasn't aggressive, but it was insistent, so I moved past as Bruin came to a halt in front of it.

"You don't want to go in?" He arched a brow at me, his dark eyes challenging.

"I'm not welcome. If you want to try, knock yourself out."

He turned toward the door, and I couldn't help but add, "No, really. Do me a favor and knock yourself out so I can explore in peace."

He rolled his eyes and braced his hands, putting his weight into trying to open what could have been a very locked door. Instead of watching him flex all of his stupid, lickable muscles, I wandered over to yet another nook carved into the wall. This one had fabric piled haphazardly on the ledge, like it had been left by someone in a hurry who planned to return to it shortly. It was soft to touch, the rich purple color as vibrant as if it had been dyed yesterday. I pulled it slowly from its resting place, flinching as something heavy hit my foot.

A book.

Spreading the fabric out, I discovered I was holding a robe. Something you would expect to see on Sarah Jessica Parker in *Hocus Pocus* as she sang to lure children to their death. Real witches didn't prey on the young and innocent.

I glanced behind me to where Mr. Meathead MC was still trying to force the door to do his bidding. Mostly. Stooping to retrieve the book, I flipped open the cover to find a neat line of handwriting stating the book I held was the *Journal of Melisande Nightshade*. The pages warmed under my hand as I flicked through them, noting each was filled with carefully formed words written in a beautiful cursive hand. Toward the center, one page was folded haphazardly, the paper bent and bent again as though it had been closed in a rush. I flipped to it, gently smoothing it flat and paused at the messy scrawl. *We who are Cursed.*

"What do you have there?"

The deep voice startled me. Whipping the book behind my back, I sprung to my feet, spinning to face the very definition of frenemy.

"Nothing. Did the door defeat you? Try giving it a good kick to show it who's boss."

"Funny." He narrowed his eyes at me, taking a step closer.

"I found a couple of grimoires stacked over there. Thought it might come in handy if you're searching for a curse breaker."

I glanced in the direction he pointed, wondering if he could be right, then flinched as he took another step that officially invaded my personal space.

"Look at me being all helpful and shit. Now, why don't you tell me what you got there?"

I wanted to hate how I had to crane my neck to keep eye contact, but the way his breath ghosted over my lips warmed me in unwelcome, yet thrilling ways. Perhaps it had been too long since I last got laid, if every man I came across made me want to jump their bones, but I was woman enough to admit that both Kylen and Bruin did it for me. An image of both of them 'doing it for me' at the same time flitted through my mind, and I forced myself to take a step back.

Clearing my throat and decidedly ignoring how damp my panties seemed to have become, I turned under the guise of continuing my search. A large hand wrapped around my bicep, and in the next instant, my back hit the stone wall. Bruin boxed me in, standing so close my nipples brushed his chest as I inhaled sharply, ready to let loose with an acerbic remark. The words froze on my tongue as he dropped his lips to my ear.

"You're the one who wanted us to play nice, Sparky. And I can be very nice if I want to be. I could make your last days mind-numbingly fucking wonderful right up until I kill you. I bet you'd even thank me for it. Now tell me, little witch"—he tucked a finger under my chin, lifting my face so his lips hovered a whisper above mine—"Are you wet for me?"

Every cell in my body wanted to nod. To let him lift me against the wall so I could ride him hard. Especially as he flexed his hips, pressing his hard length against my stomach and proving he was ready and willing.

But that would be letting him win.

Instead, I gave a rude snort and slid out from under him, hiding the wobble in my legs as I caught a whiff of fresh air. The catacombs felt too crowded, and I prayed that wherever the air was coming from, it would give me some space to escape the building attraction I had to the last person I wanted to be with.

And the first person I desperately wanted to rail me.

Bruin

*W*HAT THE FUCK *was I doing?*

The thought occurred to me as I adjusted my erection and followed the bitch, who happened to be a witch, whom I had been sent to kill. The Grim Hearts MC wasn't a club you messed with. You came for one of us? We all came for you. And no one walked away from that.

So why had I agreed to this side quest to the middle of nowhere instead of getting my job done and heading back to the fold?

The answer to that lay in the fizzing power in my veins that had gone from a simmer to a boil since Little Miss Sparkle Fingers had decided to fuck up my life. I could feel the pull of the tide before the scent of the ocean told me we were headed for an exit. I could sense pockets of water within the catacombs where the ocean had eroded the rock over centuries. While my power predominantly gave me control over the weather, the boost I was experiencing seemed to give me a deeper connection to my element than I'd ever had before.

Whether it was the town itself, or the witch who'd brought me here, remained to be seen.

Dust tickled my nose, threatening to send me into a sneezing fit as I broke into a jog, only slowing to a walk when Harlow's perfectly plump ass came into view. I wanted to bite it. Leave my marks all over her body and watch as she broke apart, begging for my cock. I imagined those sassy lips stretched around my girth as I fucked into her mouth. Tears leaking down her face as she gagged while begging me for more with those expressive eyes.

Unbidden, a new image broke into the fantasy.

This time it was me on my knees. My lips stretched wide. Me gagging on... Fucking Kylen.

Alone in the hotel room the previous night, he'd acted completely unaware of what he was doing when he'd stripped naked in front of me to change for bed, but his vines had given him away. Those wandering ropes of greenery tightened over my cock, even as they slid along my crack. Teasing. Waiting. I hadn't missed the sly look he'd thrown me as I'd grown hard under the covert ministrations. He wanted me. I hated to admit it, but I wanted him, too. Shame the whole fucking, then killing his friend thing was going to put a dampener on our budding romance.

My cell phone burned a hole in my pocket, willing me to make contact with the club and give the update they were expecting hours ago. How could I tell them the plan had encountered a little SNAFU. Situation normal: all fucked up. I sighed. Normally, I was the reliable one. The guy who got shit done, and damn the consequences, because my club was all that mattered. I was still that guy. Just... hornier?

Barely suppressing a groan of frustration, I turned a corner and stepped out into daylight.

"Holy shit." The words escaped me on a breath that was a little too reverent to be good for my reputation.

The dusty floor gave way to pure white sand beneath my

boots, and I felt the strongest urge to ditch my shoes and socks so I could feel the powder-soft grains between my toes. We were in a cove. A small beach tucked away from the coast with high cliff faces sheltering it on three sides. The gray-green waves lapped gently at the shore, and a sense of absolute peace lightened my heart for the first time in a long time. To my right, the river launched itself from the cliff in a joyous waterfall, causing the meeting of fresh and salt water in the shallows nearby.

Harlow was down at the ocean's edge, her dark head bent over whatever she'd hidden from me in the catacombs. It looked like a book of some kind. What was she up to? Despite my growing physical attraction to her, I didn't trust her.

A shout from above brought her head up and around, a smile growing on her face as she stepped away from the water. Breaking my gaze away from her, I glanced up to find Kylen and Addie on the cliff.

"Be careful up there," Harlow called.

Addie danced along the edge, pretending to lose her balance and falling back into the grass before she sprang to her feet and repeated the game. Harlow's warm chuckle floated over to me on the breeze. It was clear to anyone how much she loved that kid. It was going to be a complication.

As though the thought of my job here had summoned them, my phone buzzed in my pocket. Shit, I couldn't put it off anymore, so as subtly as I could, I moved toward the waterfall and slipped the device out of my pocket, connecting the call.

"Hey, what's up? I can't talk long."

"Why the fuck have you been radio silent? Is the bitch dead yet?" Kevin's voice was an annoying mix of surly and sullen, and I had to bite back the sharp retort rising on my tongue.

In the last twenty-four hours I'd been electrocuted, bound by grope-y vines, shoved in a trunk, kidnapped, and cock teased all in the name of his ego. I loved my brothers, but sometimes they really pissed me off.

"Good to hear from you, Kev. It's been too long. How's the shiner?"

He really hadn't liked wearing a black eye given to him by a woman. The torrent of curse words that came back at me brought a dangerous smile to my lips. He ran out of steam a couple of seconds later, and with a final "fuck", he redirected the conversation.

"Seeing as you haven't bothered to check in, I'm calling for an update, *brother*."

The term of endearment was gritted out, as though he were picturing my demise right alongside my target's. We'd always had a love-hate relationship, but being legacies, neither of us were willing to let shit get in the way of the club. So, for the club, I'd do my fucking job.

Behind me, Harlow was still preoccupied with Addie and Kylen. Good. Using the roar of the waterfall to cover my voice, I pressed closer to the cliff face and hoped they didn't notice me gone until I finished the call.

"We hit a snag during recon and had to detour to this place called Spells Hollow. You heard of it? It's a middle of nowhere ghost town that feels like there's magic in the ground. Everything is on track, and the job will go off without a hitch."

"Heading to bumfuck nowhere with your mark instead of putting a bullet in her brain sounds like a pretty big fucking hitch to me."

I rolled my eyes at his dramatics. "Either way, dead is dead, and it's going to happen. I'll call you when it's done."

"I expect a postcard with her corpse on the front within the next week."

I snorted. "I doubt that will make it through the mail, but I'll see what I can do."

Kevin grunted, clearly missing the sarcasm in my voice. "Just get it done. You have one week before I call for your patch for betraying the club." The call disconnected before I could curse him out for abusing his power as president. Fuck. How did this all go so sideways?

"Whatcha doing?"

I spun to find Harlow watching me with hard eyes. Her long body stretched out in a lean against the cliff face with her arms crossed tightly across her chest. My heart kicked at the sight of her, even as my stomach dropped at how much she could have heard.

"Because it kinda seems like you might have been going back on our deal. Were you betraying me, Bruin?"

The best defense was always a good offense, and my cock was well on board as I stepped into her body, crowding her against the cliff face.

"Nothing's changed with our deal, Sparky. You have nothing to worry about."

Her hands rested on my chest, and the electricity dancing over the tips of her fingers prickled my skin through my shirt and sent zaps of lust straight to my balls. This attraction I had was wild. She was a fighter. A warrior. I liked that too damn much. Especially since it was that quality that had gotten her into this mess in the first place.

Sliding my thigh between her legs, I dropped my lips to her ear.

"If you're up for some side benefits while we're alone down here, I won't say no." I squeezed her hip, closing my eyes to drink in the small sound she made in response to my teasing. "It would feel so good."

She shivered as I ran my nose up her neck, breathing in her scent. My body tightened, eager to get her beneath me as I slowly ran my hands up her sides.

"What are you doing to me?" she whispered, her lips a breath away from my own.

"Anything you want me to." I should have been concerned by how much I meant the statement, but I was preoccupied by how well her body fit against mine. How her soft curves perfectly contrasted against my hard muscles.

"How about..."

I leaned in closer, ready to fulfill any fantasy she had. Hell, all of them. In alphabetical order. All the way from vanilla to kink.

The dreamy look dropped from her face.

"How about you stop plotting my murder behind my back and keep out of my way?"

With a strong shove, she slipped her body out from beneath mine and stormed back toward the entrance to the catacombs.

August 27th, 1654

Mother has predicted a blood moon in the skies tonight, which means I'll shortly be leaving my old life behind me. By sunrise tomorrow, I'll be the high priestess of Spells Hollow.

The townspeople are giddy for tonight's ceremony. I've never seen them this way outside of our seasonal celebrations, nor had this much wine available since the summer solstice. But Mother insists this is a time for merriment.

My nerves say otherwise. After all, Spells Hollow is a truly special coven.

Before Mother became high priestess, it was my grandmother who founded our little town. Unwilling to deny her magic and live in fear of persecution, she fled France with her newborn daughter. She used to say this land called to her like a siren, and so she built her home here, adopting the name Nightshade.

More witches joined her over the years. Powerful families from all over England, Ireland, and Spain who felt unsafe in their homes. They all were welcomed by my grandmother. Even humans settled with them, part of the secret and protection of the new coven. All led by my family.

As the first of the Nightshade line to be born in Spells Hollow since the founding of the town, expectations are high. My connection to this land is the strongest in the coven. They truly believe I will lead us into a new era of light.

I fear they have misplaced their faith.

Despite preparing for this day my whole life, I never thought it would happen this quickly. I'm only in my sixteenth year. If it were not for Mother's condition, I would insist on continuing my training first. Leading the coven is a sacred duty. I do not take the calling lightly, nor do I feel ready at this time, but it seems the fates have their plans. Mother does not have long left, and she wishes to induct me into the role herself, before it is too late.

It is an honor to have her support, even for a short while. I'll covet every scrap of knowledge from her and use it to guide me as much as possible. Truthfully, I envy my mother. She had my grandmother as her advisor for twenty years. We only returned her to the earth three years ago, and the memories still pain my heart and the hearts of the many who treasured her.

I don't know how I'll fare when Mother succumbs. I'll have the town elders, but none of them has truly led the coven. They've never had the future of the town resting on their adolescent shoulders. Verity and Royce think I can handle it, but doubt creeps into my mind and spins its twisted web. I find myself trapped in thoughts of failure, destroying the legacy of the Nightshade witches before me.

I'm haunted by dreams of the town in flames, curses consuming my people as my loved ones scream for me. They should have been safe here. I should have been able to protect them.

How can I shoulder this burden alone? Without my mother or grandmother to guide me, I'll need people I trust. Not just the elders, but people I choose for qualities I value. If I'm to bring about an era of prosperity, I shall embrace the changes necessary to grow this coven.

After tonight, Spells Hollow will be my town. I can feel the sun setting, giving rise to the blood moon, calling me to my power and my people. I don't feel ready for this, not at all, but I believe in the guiding hand of the land my ancestors chose.

It's time for everything to change.

12

Harlow

I blew out a breath, closing the cover of Melisande's journal and leaning back on my hands. My feet dangled over the cliff edge, the expanse of air below them a small thrill as I breathed deeply. Below me, seagulls pinwheeled over the water, calling to each other before diving into the wash of the waves over and over. Something about the sea air had the electricity that crackled in my veins feeling both stronger and slightly less wild than normal. Melisande wrote of her connection to the land, and the odd sense that I could feel the link, too, rode me hard.

Why had I been brought here?

While we explored the town the day before, I'd held my breath, waiting for... something to tell me what I had to do. The fact that twenty-four hours later I still wasn't any closer to learning the answer was setting me on edge. An hour earlier I'd snapped at Addie for something ridiculous that had already slipped my mind and had to excuse myself to cool my head with the ocean breeze. Kylen had been a godsend since we arrived in the town, encouraging Addie to get outside and hunt for the elusive plant he'd been searching for, leaving Lindsay free to scour the house for any information that could be of use.

My mind drifted back to Melisande's diary entry. She'd taken over the coven when she'd been sixteen, and even then, she'd known it would be destroyed. You didn't have to travel far in Spells Hollow to spot the fire damage and decay of a broken community. The most disconcerting thing was in the first line. The blood moon heralded her change in fate. Was it a coincidence? I desperately wanted to think so, but unfortunately, magic loved its signs and preordained destinies. As much as I would have loved to play ostrich, it wouldn't have done me any favors. Despite the warmth of the day, a cold shiver worked down my spine.

Suddenly, my position on the edge of the cliffs felt too exposed. With a glance around to ensure I was still alone out on the grass, I found my feet and decided to check in on Lindsay. Bruin had spent the morning trying to break into the other houses in town, but last I'd checked, he hadn't had much luck. I wondered if his plan was to pillage and plunder while he was biding his time to take me out. Not that I cared about his plans outside of surviving the ones involving me dead.

That was future-Harlow's problem, though. Present-Harlow needed to see if her bestie was going to do what he did best and save her ass.

"Honey, I'm home," I called as I stepped into the cool interior of the house with a smirk pulling at my cheek.

"Hey, Harls, I'm upstairs. Come up here. I think you need to see this."

"That sounds ominous." The bottom step creaked beneath my shoe as I ascended to the first floor.

"Where are you?"

"In here."

I followed his voice to my left and found him in a dusty

room with wall-to-wall shelving and a heavy desk sitting in front of a brick fireplace. The shelves were full of books. Leather-bound volumes with gold detailing that looked hand painted.

"If you're looking for shiny things, you should have gone looting with Bruin," I joked, stepping up beside my bestie, who seemed focused on the book in his hand.

"What's up?"

Lindsay shook himself, as though coming out of a trance, and cast me an indecipherable look. I furrowed my brow, waiting for him to say something, but instead of answering, he handed the book to me.

It was immediately evident that I was holding a grimoire. Even without reading what was written on the pages, I felt the shift of energy. The volume was almost too hot to touch, a fact so distracting that it took me a moment to notice I was looking at a family tree of some sort. Generations of names branched out cross the pages documenting births, marriages and deaths.

"This is pretty cool," I said, still not sure what was making Lindsay so damn twitchy.

He hadn't even made a joke about hitting on Bruin when I brought him up. He grunted, pointing at a name in the middle of the page.

"Donahue Torann," I read.

Doing some quick math, I realized his birth date was three-hundred and ninety years ago. Beside his name on one side, it showed his relationship with Melisande Nightshade, on the other, his sibling, Levina. According to the tree, Melisande and Donahue had died in the same year, and the cause of death was noted as the same. *Curse*. Levina had survived ten years past that. She had a partner listed and children branching off beneath. A shiver ran through me.

Under cause of death, she also had the word curse. Backtracking, I confirmed that their mother had died of natural causes, and their father by gunshot, but every generation after Donahue Torann had succumbed to only one form of death.

"What does this mean?" I asked, tracing over the word as it appeared again and again on every branch of the tree down to the last entry. Harlow Davis.

"What the f—?" I jerked violently, barely avoiding dropping the book as the shock of seeing my own name on the page sank in. I'd heard of enchanted family trees like this, but never seen one. They weren't exactly common in foster homes.

As I stared, trying to process the development, a fine line extended to the side of my name and forked several times.

"Nope. Nopenopenopenope." I shoved the book at Lindsay and turned to leave, freezing in place at the sight of a portrait hanging beside the door I'd entered through.

The figures in the portrait wore clothes that would have been modern at the time Spells Hollow was a thriving community. The man had been painted wearing a white shirt and brown vest, while the woman was in a dress suited to a renaissance faire. The man's dark hair was tousled, and the artist had managed to capture a wicked glint in his eye and a lift to his lips that made him seem roguish and approachable all at once. My eyes slid over to the woman again, despite my wishes. She had the same dark hair. Her eyes looked similar to her brother's, but the comparison was insignificant seeing as she looked identical to another person in the room.

"Why is there a painting of you in ye' olde garb?" Lindsay asked, moving toward the portrait for a closer look.

"This is too much," I muttered, striding from the room and hitting the stairs at a run.

"Harls, wait."

Lindsay's voice followed me out the front door, but I couldn't wait. I had to get out. To get away and clear my head.

"Where are you going?" Bruin paused in the process of hefting a chair at the front window of the house next door, but I had no words for him.

"Stop her," Lindsay yelled at the biker, but I wasn't in the mood to sit in a sharing circle and sing Kumbaya.

Electricity skated over my skin, zapping Bruin as he made a grab for me.

"No way am I getting electrocuted again because she has it in her head to do something stupid."

"Harlow." The panic in Lindsay's voice broke through my need for escape long enough for me to force a deep breath.

"Get the others and head back to the motel. I need to clear my head, so I'm going to walk back. I'll see you soon."

"But—"

"It's fine. I'm the strong one, remember?" I held up my hand in demonstration, then turned on my heel and stalked into the woods.

Images of family trees and doppelgangers consumed my mind as I skirted trees and stepped over rubble. As an orphan, I'd never felt like I belonged anywhere. To anyone. And now a blood moon vision had sent me to the home of my ancestors? It was too bizarre to process, and I found myself wishing for the mother I never knew. I'd been too scared to look at her name on the tree. I knew how she'd died... at least how they'd told me she did. The idea it could have been this curse instead? Nope. It wasn't the time to open that can of worms.

I lost track of the path as I wove my way deeper into the woods, led by my thoughts more than my feet, and it wasn't until I realized the light had dimmed significantly that I stopped to look around. An unnatural twilight descended around me, stealing the sun's light despite the fact it couldn't have been later than three in the afternoon. Shadows reached across the ground toward me as the insect sounds cut off abruptly. Flexing my hands, I allowed a trickle of power to dance across my fingertips as I waited to see what would emerge from the darkness. The snap of a stick brought my head around, and I caught a glimpse of movement beyond the dark trees.

"Come out, come out," I muttered and planted my feet wide, ready to fight.

A chuffing sound came from my left at the same time leaves rustled to my right. Shit, how many of them were there? I raised a hand, ready to send out a warning strike and hopefully dissuade whatever creature had decided to try me.

At the last moment, movement in my peripheral vision made me swing my arm around and release a solid bolt of electricity at what looked like a giant gray wolf. The beast didn't even slow as he launched himself at me.

We crashed to the ground in a pile of limbs, and I winced as my skull bounced on the packed dirt. My ears rang, vision blurring as I tried to dislodge the heavy mass of fur growling in my face. Saliva hung from its muzzle in long drops as the beast opened its maw. I tried to shock the thing again but gasped in pain as the wolf flexed its paws, digging its claws into my flesh as it lowered its head and growled.

What kind of animal was immune to magic?

I could be in real trouble here.

I began to struggle in earnest, kicking at the ground as I tried to work my arms out from under the beast, but froze as a deep growl rumbled to my right. The sound was deeper and far more menacing than the wolf had made, but my body responded by going completely lax. Maybe I'd hit my head harder than I thought. Or maybe this was the curse all my family succumbed to. My family. The most inappropriate giggle bubbled out from between my lips at the thought of finally finding out who I belonged to, only to die, just like the rest of them.

I closed my eyes, sending up a silent apology to Lindsay and Addie as the wolf's foul breath ghosted over my face. Something soft brushed against my skin, then I could take a full breath again. Cracking my eyes open despite the throbbing in my head, I was faced with the sight of a huge white wolf facing off against my attacker. The gray wolf growled as it sank onto its haunches and sprang forward, but the white wolf effortlessly absorbed its attack, swiping at its face until blood dripped from its paws.

The scene began to blur as my heartbeat pounded in my ears, and the last thing I saw as consciousness slipped away was the gray wolf turning tail while the white wolf stretched up onto two legs, taking on a masculine form. Sunlight flared in my eyes, blinding me for a moment before everything turned black.

Ranto

SMALL ROCKS and sticks stabbed at my bare feet as I stumbled over to the unconscious female on the ground, cursing my vulnerable human form. A warm breeze brushed against my naked skin, and I resisted the urge to shift and regain my protective layer of fur. I'd spent too long in my wolf form this time around, and it would take me a while to adjust to the discomfort of my human form, but I couldn't find it in me to regret it. Not when the single most important being in the world was finally close enough to touch.

I'd accepted the job to investigate the Grim Hearts MC on a whim. As a PI, most of my work consisted of proving cases of embezzlement and infidelity. But when your best friend from the police academy calls you up with a chance to help bring down one of the most notorious crime organizations in the state? Sign me the hell up. The fact that it would mean going an indeterminate amount of time without having to take candid shots of old, rich, white guys' naked asses as they pounded their social-climbing secretaries into the desk was just an added bonus.

I never dreamed I'd finally come face to face with my mate.

Her dark hair fell across surprisingly delicate features,

relaxed in a way that would have been endearing if she weren't unconscious. As the wind changed direction, it brought with it a scent I was becoming very familiar with, even if it had been faint due to the distance I had imposed upon myself up to this point. She smelled like night-blooming flowers and the secrets of the moon. A combination that dulled my senses to the point of insanity while simultaneously drawing me in to meet my doom.

My primary objective had been deserted after her confrontation with the president of the MC. No longer interested in their destruction, my only goal had become the protection of my mate and her pack. A chosen family that had continued to grow while I watched from afar. Following Harlow had been an action I could justify as a way to isolate the club's enforcer and extract information, but staying in the shadows, playing guardian angel, had been harder to reason my way out of. I just wanted to be close to her. This level of interference had never been in the plan.

Her eyelids fluttered, the movement pulling me out of my reverie as I drew close enough to touch her for the first time.

"I've got you. You're safe," I murmured, sliding my arms beneath her shoulders and knees, and hoisting her against my body.

Part of me hoped she would remain unconscious a little longer so I could avoid the awkward conversation about my nakedness, while the other half was desperate to hear her speak directly to me. To hold her attention for just a moment.

This deep in the woods, it was a risk to carry her all the way back to the road alone and in my human form. There were many things that stalked beneath the tree canopy that would happily make a meal out of the both of us, and I couldn't trust my luck to hold that whatever attacked next would be easy enough to fight off and protect her at the same time. I'd been lucky with the wolf. I might not be able to manage it again, and losing her wasn't an option. Instead, I turned my head toward the campsite I'd slept at the previous night, with a very surly gryphon for company.

The scent of wood fire reached me long before we arrived at the clearing where Hendrix sat on a camp chair, auburn curls obscuring his face as he stared at the ground between his knees. I made no effort to hide our approach, but he didn't bother to lift his head until we were almost toe to toe.

"You should be careful. There are wolves out here, you know," he murmured, eyeing my mate's lax form.

A growl rolled over my tongue before I could swallow it, causing his gaze to flick to mine. "I know."

A moment passed, each of us eyeing the other as I waited to see his reaction to my current situation. Wolves in general got a bad rap, and I couldn't even blame people for it, considering one was responsible for what happened to my mate. Granted, there was a big difference between other wolves and raiju, but most people weren't educated in the different species. I wanted Hendrix to like me. The funny thing was, he seemed to be more cautious of my human form than he was of my canine.

"What you got there?" he asked eventually, flicking his gaze back to my mate.

"She hit her head and lost consciousness. Do you have a first aid kit?"

He reached into the backpack and began unloading things. "Lay her down. I'll take a look at what we're dealing with here."

Another growl snuck out, and heat rose in my cheeks at the possessiveness in the sound. It was definitely something I'd have to work on. Witches were renowned for having multiple mates, and as much as the idea of sharing made me want to tear shit up, the man in me recognized the benefits of having multiple men to keep her safe and happy.

"Easy there, Fido. I'm dealing with your literal swinging dick here. Don't make me put up with the metaphorical one, too."

I snorted. "I'm comfortable with my sexuality, and how the hell are you so prudish when you're a shifter?"

"I can keep my clothing on with my shift, thank you very much. I'm civilized like that."

Whatever.

Magic was freaking weird, and the idea of clothing disappearing and reappearing as a person shifted creeped me out. Seriously, where did it go? Would Hendrix cough up lint balls from his clothing being absorbed into his skin with a shift? Or did it hang above his form and somehow not get ripped to shreds like mine did if I wore it through the shift? My head hurt thinking about it.

"Please don't burst a blood vessel thinking too hard. Make yourself useful and prop her up so I can see her head."

Between us, we got her into position and confirmed that while a large, purpling lump was forming on the base of her skull, there was no wound to tend. It was as we were laying her out flat that her breathing hitched, and she slowly opened her eyes.

Her brow furrowed. "Naked man?"

Oh shit. I cupped a hand over my cock and backed up a step to give her room, concerned for the first time that I should have at least tried to find some clothing. Unfortunately, my carry bag was somewhere back in the woods, abandoned the second I saw her in danger.

"Sorry."

"It's okay. Just a surprise to wake up to a strange penis in my face."

The penis in question kicked in response to her attention, and I subtly tried to press it into submission. There would be plenty of time for them to be acquainted in the future, preferably when she hadn't just regained consciousness.

Hendrix's deep chuckle stole her attention, and I tried to hide the way my lip wanted to curl in warning. Hendrix was a friend. Kind of. He'd helped me. More importantly, he'd helped her.

"It's you."

Okay, there was no part of me that liked the breathless awe that those two words held. Hendrix shifted back on his heels, flicking a quick look at me before grunting and pushing to stand.

"He was worried about you. I'll give you both some space."

Much to my relief, he crawled into his tent and zipped the opening closed, at least giving us the illusion of privacy.

"How are you feeling?" I asked, unable to resist edging closer to her again.

"I'm fine. I mean, I've got a killer headache and could use some water, but I'm alive and breathing. So, yeah..."

I nodded, eyeing the bag Hendrix had left beside his abandoned chair. Hell, maybe he had something I could cover up with to make my mate feel a bit more comfortable.

Turned out, the best I could find was a towel to wrap around my hips. The water flask I found a moment later made me feel like crowing, and I presented it to her as though it were a precious jewel.

She accepted it with a thanks and tipped her head back, throat working as she swallowed again and again. Damn, that was hot. As she finally dropped her arm, I made myself busy packing the bag back up and returning it to its original spot.

"Was it you?"

I paused, wondering what she was referring to.

"The wolf. Dog. Whatever. Are you the one who has been following us?"

Nothing in her tone told me what she wanted the answer to be, so I went with the truth.

"I didn't mean to scare you. A raiju's mate means everything to them. You were an...unexpected discovery during a job, and I found it impossible to stay away."

Those dark brows furrowed. Maybe I should have been more subtle or given her some kind of platitude until she was fully healed, but now that I'd decided to try for the mate bond, I found myself impatient to get closer.

"Wait. So when you say... Wait. You said mate? Ugh. My head hurts." Confusion shone in her as she held a hand to her forehead, and despite the voice in my head screaming to give her space, my mouth ignored the good advice.

"Orgasms are good for headaches." Way to not make things weird.

"Not always true." Hendrix's unwelcome input came from inside his tent.

"Shut it, gryphon."

"Bite me, wolf."

"Raiju." I sniffed. He knew the difference, the asshole.

The insult was forgotten as I turned back to see a blinding smile stretch over my mate's face. Even better, as she shifted her legs, I caught the unmistakable scent of arousal. Yes! A deep breath to calm myself did nothing but encourage my growing erection as more of her delicious scent filled my lungs.

"So... I'm your mate," she said, rolling onto her knees and closing the distance between us.

I nodded, worried any movement would scare her off.

"And you want to make me feel better."

I bobbed my head faster. Hell yes, I'd do anything for her.

"Well, in the absence of Tylenol, it seems like the best option."

I dragged her to me, inhaling her last word as my mouth crashed against hers. Lightning cracked over my skin, making me shiver as I absorbed the charge. My cock ached for her, and I mentally reminded it that this time was for her. And only for her. With careful hands, I laid her back on the ground and made quick work of her pants and underwear, pointedly ignoring the frustrated groan from inside the tent.

"Do you have to do that right here?"

"Put your headphones on. We're about to get loud."

My mate snorted at the cheeky grin I sent her, but the sound transformed into a long groan as I dipped my head and licked a long line up her pussy. Her taste exploded on my tongue, and I had to take a moment to reach down and squeeze the hell out of my cock to keep from coming on the spot. Fuck, she was spectacular. Her fingers threaded through my long white hair, and I grinned in delight as she tightened her grip to the point of pain and pulled my mouth back where she needed it.

Alternating between hard flicks over her nub and long, indulgent strokes, I worked her until she was squirming beneath me before spearing my tongue into her heat over and over. Her scent surrounded me, pulling me deeper and deeper under her spell as the world around faded to black. My cock wept into the dirt beneath us as my body warmed to the lightning she sent through my veins.

Just when the sensations felt too overwhelming, she threw her head back, screaming through an earth-shattering orgasm as our mate link clicked into place. I groaned, unable to stop lapping at her as my cock kicked hard, my release painting the earth in sticky white stripes.

"That was..." she breathed, cutting off as another tremor shook her sensitive body.

I hummed, nuzzling her core and taking another lick, smiling against her flesh as she shuddered again.

"Stop."

"But I want another one." I was whining, but there was no part of me that wanted to let up.

"Play your cards right, and I'll let you do it again soon. Maybe when we don't have an audience." She cut her eyes toward the tent.

"Don't mind me. You certainly didn't care a few minutes ago." Hendrix's voice was slightly strangled, and a small sniff gave me all the information I needed.

"Don't think I can't smell what you just did, gryphon."

A muffled curse was his only response.

"What...?"

"Let's just say mine isn't the only cum scent in my nose right now."

My mate's face darkened to a pretty pink shade. Speaking of...

"I'm Ranto, by the way. We haven't really had the opportunity to introduce ourselves."

"Harlow. Though I'd say we're nailing the getting-to-know-you thing."

I couldn't help but agree. I knew how she tasted, the way her face twisted when she came, the needy little sounds she made... I cleared my throat, adjusting the towel that did little to hide my rallying cock. He was a trooper. Especially with our new mate bond in place.

We exchanged dopey grins until her attention caught on the now-dark sky.

"Shit."

I suppressed a whimper as she jumped to her feet and pulled her underwear and pants back up her legs.

"Everyone will be stressing out. I have to get back."

"I'm going with you."

She paused, an assessing look crossing her face for a moment before she finished zipping her pants.

"Deal. Besides, you need some clothes if you're staying in your human form, and my bestie happens to have brought enough to stock a Macy's."

I swept a hand out graciously, relieved that I didn't have to keep following her in the shadows. I would have, if she said no, but this way I could stay close enough to look after her properly.

"Lead the way."

With a deep breath, she slapped the top of the tent and strode toward the trees. "See you, dude. Thanks for the hospitality."

A grunt came from inside, and I grinned at his stubbornness.

"Thanks, Hendrix. See you around." Without waiting for a response, I trotted after Harlow with a new bounce in my step. I was naked, trekking through the woods in a towel, but I was with my mate, and soon I'd meet her whole pack.

Life was good.

14

Kylen

"She should be back by now," Lindsay muttered as he paced lines into the cheap motel carpet.

This was the first time I'd seen him really worked up. Even when Bruin was chasing us down on the highway, Lindsay was cool and in control. Hell, he'd wanted popcorn when Harlow was fighting! He clearly knew when Harlow wasn't in any danger, and this...may not be one of those times.

No one had been happy to let Harlow roam the woods alone, but what could we do? She wasn't the type to let someone tell her what to do, and none of us were the type to manhandle someone into obeying. Except maybe Bruin. But there had been something off about him since he explored the catacombs with her yesterday. He'd been lying on his bed, glaring at the ceiling ever since we got back today. Hadn't spoken a word to anyone. I couldn't tell if he was plotting something, or just pissed he'd finally let Harlow out of sight. Possibly both.

Lindsay continued to pace between the bedroom window, the open door to the other room, and the main door leading outside, constantly checking the peephole for any signs of the missing lightning witch. Addie followed him with her eyes from where she'd curled up in the armchair, concern lacing her young features. Every few seconds, she'd check her phone—an early iPhone model, by the looks of it, with more scratches than Harlow's car.

Grabbing my trusty backpack from beside the bed, I rummaged around until I pulled out a beat-up deck of cards. "Anybody up for a game?"

Addie's eyes lit up, and she bounced over to sit at the end of my bed. "Ooh, yes!"

"Bad idea," Lindsay commented from beside the window, smirking at Addie. "She's a grifter. Harlow taught her a few years back and now flat-out refuses to play her."

"I can't help that I have trustworthy eyes and very little remorse, Lins."

"Eh, I might give you a run for your money, kiddo." I grinned as I started shuffling the worn cards. "How do you think I've afforded to stay on the road so long?"

She scoffed. "Bullshit. You don't even look that old."

I chuckled. "Thank you. But I've been traveling with my research since the day I graduated college, so it's been a few years."

"Oh, don't be shy," Bruin taunted from his bed. "Share with the class."

"I will if you join us for a few games," I offered, holding up the cards like an olive branch.

We'd left him untied since yesterday, which was probably for the best. The way my mind wandered when he was around was dangerous, especially when he was tangled in my vines. I'd said they have a mind of their own, which is only mostly true. I don't have to be actively in control of them all the time. But when I'm not concentrating, their actions reflect on my mind. And my attractions. I really hope they didn't try anything with Bruin. I'd at least like to trust someone before groping them with plants.

Bruin raised an eyebrow, unimpressed by the invitation.

Unable to resist the challenge of his attitude, I stepped over to his bed and whispered in his ear, low enough to prevent the others from overhearing, "Be a good boy now, and stop brooding. Harlow will be back soon for you to antagonize her. Play with us until then."

His jaw ticked, as I imagine he scanned through the many ways he could kill me for that. But I had to take the risk. There was something so enticing about him, I wanted to know more. And I think he did, too.

"Fine." He growled. "You're on."

"Yes! Haha!" Addie cackled. "Looks like mama's gonna have a shiny new bike by the end of the night!"

He stood with a dramatic sigh, probably to distract her from the redness creeping up his neck. "Keep dreaming, kid. Hope you've won enough from your friends to pay me off by the time I'm through with you."

Lindsay snorted. "Destroy him, Addie."

Not if I destroy him another way first.

We sat in a small circle on my bed, and I dealt out the cards for a five-card draw. While Lindsay gave Addie a quick pep talk about how to take everything Bruin had and leave him with nothing but his underwear and tears, I looked over at the biker. He was intriguing. Not my usual type at all when it came to men, but his fierce attitude drew me in, much like Harlow's. I couldn't say if I wanted to tame it or let it consume me.

While I checked my cards, I told him, "I'm twenty-seven, by the way."

He didn't look up from his cards, but his posture softened a little. "So you've been traveling for what... five years? Not bad."

As Lindsay predicted, Addie quickly dominated each

round. Seriously, the girl was something else. She could pass a lie detector test as easily as ordering a coffee. No wonder she had Harlow and Lindsay wrapped around her little finger.

"Jesus, kid." Bruin mourned another defeat. "If I ever need someone to lie on the stand for me, I'm calling you first."

She smiled sweetly as she retrieved another fifty dollars and added it to her winnings. "I know I'm a good liar, but trust I'm telling the truth when I say this: If you do anything to hurt Harlow, you'll want to keep me very far away from government officials."

He watched her suspiciously, and I could swear I saw the faintest glimmers of respect and a smidge of fear in his dark eyes. "Noted."

Bruin was smart to be careful around Addie. Magic or not, she could be a lot of trouble for him if he planned to carry out his threats. If anything happened to Harlow, Lindsay would need help keeping her from going after him, and I'd be the first volunteer.

"She was so freaked out earlier. It's weird seeing her like that." Addie frowned, deep in thought, before she looked up at me. "Do you think that girl in the drawing is really one of Harlow's ancestors? Is that why she was called here?"

"Maybe, yeah," I answered, thinking of the books Lindsay found. "A lot of spells in the grimoires were storm related, and it's hard to deny that resemblance, even in a painting. Does Harlow know anything about her family history?"

Addie shook her head. "Nothing, same as me and Lindsay. We're all from the same under-funded orphanage of abandoned magical brats. Well, mostly magical."

Lindsay sighed, finally turning away from the window. "Actually, that's not entirely true."

"What are you talking about?"

"Not about your magic. Sorry, Ads, that one's still a

mystery. But we do know something about Harlow's mom." He dragged the wooden desk chair over and took a seat close to Addie. "Harlow got a call when we were...must've been around nine or so. Her mom had just died in jail."

"She never told me that." Addie's voice was barely above a whisper.

He gave her a sympathetic smile. "She doesn't like to talk about it because she never really knew her mom. I don't think she even remembers her name. She was arrested while pregnant, so Harlow was born in jail and sent straight into the system. Kinda like you."

"My mom was in a car accident and died of her injuries after," she explained to me, her voice cracking. "Apparently, the last thing she said was for the doctors to save me instead of her. There wasn't a dad to take me home, or maybe he didn't want me, so here I am."

"He would have wanted you," I said, leaving no room for arguments. "If he'd been there, he'd have brought you home."

Addie wiped her eyes with the heel of her hand. "I dunno about that. He was probably a dirtbag who knocked up my mom and ran." She sniffed and forced a smile at me. "But thanks, it's a nice thought."

I had no idea why I felt so protective of this kid I'd only known for three days. Maybe it was because I saw how fiercely Harlow loved her. It would destroy her if anything happened to Addie. But there was also something familiar about Addie's eyes. As I stared, it finally clicked. They were the same blue as my mom's. Her right eye was even a little smaller than the other. How strange to meet someone like that here, the place where I might finally complete her research. The fates were tricky things.

After a moment, Bruin asked the question on everyone's mind. "How did Harlow's mom die?"

"At the time, we were just told there was an accident. But this was the first Harlow had ever heard about her mom. They'd never met or spoken to each other. She kept on asking and calling the prison directly but got nothing. She even started going to the library to research it." Lindsay smiled for a moment, then dropped it as he continued, "Eventually, we discovered that there was a riot that got real crazy. A few hours in, it caused some kind of electrical explosion. Her mom was right at the center of it."

The room fell silent. No one wanted to make the comparison between Harlow's magic and her mom's death, but maybe it was an accident. We had no way of knowing if it was her magic that caused the explosion. It could easily have been fate's ironic and sick sense of humor.

A creaking in the other bedroom broke the quiet, with footsteps following behind.

"What the... I thought they'd be asleep." Harlow's voice was quiet. There was a small click, then light bloomed beneath the adjoining door.

"We're in here!" Addie called out.

"Lookie who decided to finally come back." Lindsay tsked, the tension finally relaxing from his shoulders as Harlow opened the door to our room. For the first time in hours, he looked like himself. "What took you so long?"

Harlow stood in the door frame, her hair oddly mussed and dirt covering her cheeks. She looked like she'd lost a fight with a herd of cows.

Jeez, what happened to her?

"I got a little... caught up," she answered, shrugging out of her jacket with a tired smile.

A deep voice I didn't recognize spoke from behind her. "Where did you say your friend's clothes were?"

Lindsay's jaw dropped as he scampered into the other

room, pushing Harlow out of the way before yelling, "Yes, Harlow! Get some!"

Bruin and I exchanged a confused look, our curiosities piqued by the mysterious voice.

Laughter and muffled threats continued to spew from the room while Addie cautiously moved towards the door, calling out, "Harlow? What's going on in there?"

Before she could get a look inside, Harlow dashed into our room, slamming the door behind her. "Nothing your adolescent eyes need to see."

"Well, now I gotta know!"

Harlow sighed. She looked exhausted, even without the dirt on her face and leaves in her hair. "It's a long story, but his name is Ranto, and he says I'm his mate."

"As in the fated kind?" she asked. "I thought that was a shifter thing."

"Sparky, did you bring a naked man back from the woods? Are we not enough for you?" Bruin grinned mischievously.

He gestured between the two of us, and I immediately turned away to focus on packing up the cards. Why was I being brought into her possible relationships? Sure, I was definitely attracted to her, but I had no idea if she had any serious interest in me.

Harlow rolled her eyes, pointing at Bruin as she spoke. "Pretty bold to assume I'd ever consider you as an option with the whole trying-to-kill-me thing."

"Every story has its obstacles. You know my stance on the situation." He winked at her before moving to his own bed, flopping down with a grunt.

She turned to Addie, pulling her in for a tight hug and gently kissing the top of her head. "Anyway, I'm sorry for worrying you, kiddo. I didn't mean to be gone that long."

Addie hugged her back, squeezing like she was afraid

Harlow would disappear if she let go. "It's okay. You brought back a boyfriend, so I guess I understand."

"I dunno about 'boyfriend'." Harlow cringed at the word. "He got me out of a tough spot and wants to keep helping, so that's enough for me right now."

"Ooh, if he's your fated-whatever, maybe *he'll* let me get the dog!"

"Funny story. He is the dog. Wolf, actually. Raiju, technically." Harlow grinned down at her. "So, if he decides to stick around, I guess we'll see."

"What? No way! I want a do-over dog! It doesn't count if he's your boyfriend."

The door behind them opened, revealing a handsome East-Asian man in his mid-twenties, with long white hair tied up in a messy bun. He'd clearly been dressed by Lindsay; the sequined cat t-shirt and neon yellow shorts didn't look like this man's usual style.

"Hey." He smiled, showing pearly white teeth with a little extra canine. "Just wanted to say it's safe to come in now. Sorry about that."

Addie pulled away from the hug, staring at the stranger. "I have so many questions for you."

"Questions that can wait for tomorrow, kid." Harlow chuckled, giving Addie a little push into their room, before looking up at Ranto. "Do you need to rent a room, or...?"

"I'm good with a pillow on the floor. Don't worry about me." He turned to Bruin and me, giving us each a long stare, like he was trying to remember our faces from somewhere. "Uh, nice to meet you and good night."

As Ranto went back to the other room, Bruin rubbed his eyes and wordlessly walked over to the bathroom, leaving me alone with Harlow.

"Got a minute?" she asked.

I nodded, gesturing at my bed for her to sit down. "What's up?"

Taking a seat next to me, Harlow took a moment before finally speaking. "I wanted to say thank you. You've been amazing the past few days, especially with Addie. I hope we haven't held you back from your research too much, but I really appreciate everything you've done. You've turned into someone I can trust with my family, and I won't forget that."

"It's no problem at all. Addie's actually been really helpful with the research. She's collected soil samples that tell me Spells Hollow has the right components to produce the plant I'm looking for. We've made progress, and I'm quietly hopeful," I explained, excited to talk about my research. "And we were just worried about you today. Lindsay didn't say what had you so weirded out."

"That's another long story. I'll explain tomorrow, if that's okay?"

"Yeah, of course."

"Thank you." She smiled, then leaned in to brush her lips against mine in a gentle kiss that lit a fire in my chest, warming me from the inside.

Why was I reacting like a teenager? I'd kissed plenty of people before. But for some reason, kissing Harlow was different. It didn't take my breath away; it gave me the air I needed to survive. How had I lived this long not knowing what she tasted like?

She pulled away before we could take it further, her cheeks pink and pupils wide. Maybe I stood more of a chance with her than I thought.

Harlow

"SHOTGUN!"

Addie tore past me, headed for the front seat of the Camry. I snagged the hood of her sweater, smirking at the dramatic choking sound that came out of her throat.

"Forget it, squirt. You're in the back."

She huffed, giving me her best *teenage girl* look before sliding into the backseat next to Ranto. After what happened in the woods with Ranto yesterday, then my impulsive decision to kiss Kylen when we got back to the motel, I was feeling the need for some space.

I'd felt the magic of the mating bond move through me when Ranto and I were together. There was no denying it. But the draw I felt to Kylen was on a completely different level. Everything about him felt right, and even though the kiss had been a barely there brush of the lips, my magic had reached for him the same way it had for Ranto. The sound of a scuffle broke out behind me, and I turned in time to see Kylen slide into the seat before Bruin.

"Where the hell am I supposed to sit?"

I hated how attractive his scowl was. Especially when I already had more than enough guy troubles to worry about.

Kylen slapped his hands on his thighs, his shit-eating grin so wide I couldn't help but mirror it.

"Jump on, sweetheart. I'll keep you safe and sound."

"I'd rather go back in the trunk."

"That can be arranged," Lindsay sang from the driver's seat.

"Addie?" Bruin asked, dark eyes almost pleading.

In true Addie fashion, she mock-gasped, fingers lightly touching her chest as though she were truly outraged. "You expect moi, a minor, to sit on the lap of either of these strange old men? Why, Bruin, what kind of lady do you take me for?"

I snorted at her wide-eyed expression, and the way Ranto cocked his head while Kylen mouthed "old men" had me facing the front quickly to hide the laugh bubbling inside me.

"Screw this."

I jumped as the slam of the back door vibrated the entire car before the door next to me was yanked open. Without so much as an *if you please*, Bruin slid onto the front seat, lifting me into his lap. He pulled the seatbelt out, but quickly realized it wouldn't go around both of us. Instead, he buckled himself in and wrapped his arms around me, pulling me in so that my back pressed tightly to his front.

"Ready." He grunted as a low growl percolated through the interior.

A quick glance back at Ranto showed he was capable of raising his hackles, even in human form.

"It's okay," I said, even though it felt anything but, and was worsening the longer I felt Bruin's heat radiate through my clothes. Everywhere he touched burned in a way that made desire pool low in my belly.

No more men, I reminded myself firmly. Especially not one as problematic as Bruin.

Lindsay broke the awkward silence, turning over the ignition and pulling slowly out of the motel parking lot.

"The sooner we get there, the sooner we can all get out of here," he muttered as the car bumped along the unpaved road.

I studiously ignored the way the uneven surface caused my ass to bounce against Bruin's crotch in a way that felt obscene. Around the halfway mark, Bruin groaned, his hands shifting to my hips where he took a grip that bordered on painful and shifted me to straddle his thigh.

"Keep doing that and either you'll crush my balls, or I'll nut all over the seat. Maybe both."

"Sounds like a good time," Lindsay said with a small smirk as he hit another pothole and pain shot through my pelvis.

"Your leg is too hard," I groused, shifting around to find a more comfortable position.

The car jolted, and Bruin let out a squeak. Kylen and Ranto lost their composure in the backseat.

"You should have taken me up on the offer," Kylen wheezed.

"This wouldn't be a problem if you gave me back my bike." Bruin scowled at Lindsay, who grinned wider.

Thankfully, a moment later we broke through the tree line, and Spells Hollow came back into view. Despite having spent a couple of days in the ruined town, we were still no closer to working out why we had come. Lindsay pulled the car to a stop beside the town gallows, and everyone piled out, spreading out around the nearby buildings.

Instead of following the others, I climbed onto the wooden platform that looked to have weathered the years a little too well. What did it say about a town to have magically preserved gallows while the outbuildings stood in ruins? The rope of the nooses creaked as they swayed in the light breeze, the ominous sound doing nothing to lift my mood as doubt crowded in.

Forty-eight hours and all I'd learned was my ancestors had lived here and died of a curse. A blood moon had symbolized a high priestess's rise to power while it had coerced me into this vision quest thing. What the hell was I supposed to do here?

Power buzzed through my limbs as the hopelessness of my task began to weigh me down, closing my throat and making breathing difficult. I was going to die. Just like Donahue and Levina. Just like my mother. I couldn't stop it because I didn't know what *it* was. My hands shook as sparks licked at the wooden boards beneath my feet. This was all a waste of time. I should be doing something to make sure Lindsay and Addie are all right. That they will be taken care of when I'm...

Strong arms pulled me back against a hard chest, holding me up and lending strength. Electricity arced out from me in jagged forks, digging up the dirt surrounding the platform as a second set of warm hands slipped over my cheeks, tugging my head forward until I was pressed against someone else.

"We've got you. Just breathe with me." Kylen's words slipped over my lips as his fingers tightened on my jaw.

A low rumble vibrated my back, and a primitive part of me knew it was Ranto. These men, who I'd only just met, stood against my reckless power and gave me an anchor.

"Easy," Ranto soothed. Sparks danced over his arms where they tightened over my stomach. "It's like tantric sex. You gotta take your time and let the energy flow."

I huffed a laugh, then sucked in a deep breath, waiting for the moment it was safe to let go. After a few breaths, I released the energy and felt it buzz through both men, causing Kylen's blue eyes to glow neon for a moment before the air around us grew still.

"There you go. A little less orgasmic, but satisfying, nonetheless."

I elbowed Ranto, who had yet to release his grip on me.

"You horndog."

He chuckled, and a look passed briefly between him and Kylen before they both stepped back.

"Are you okay?" Kylen asked, his eyes running over me as though checking for damage.

"I'm good. Just got a little...carried away."

They both nodded as the awkwardness of the situation settled over me.

"I'm gonna go..." I trailed off, pointing toward the cliffs as both men hurried to agree and wave me off.

Whatever was happening between us was something I'd have to deal with soon, but for right now, I would do what any self-preserving woman would: escape real life by sticking my nose in a book.

April 25th, 1660

Every day, it becomes clearer to me that I could never have done any of this alone.

It wasn't intentional, of course, a lover from each of the nine leading families in Spells Hollow. The elders were most affronted. Verity insisted on being present for my last four announcements to our council, and, oh, how she laughed at them more each time.

What would Mother say about all this? I've asked myself that a thousand times, but I believe she would be happy for me, despite my unconventional methods. She saw how Royce and I fell for each other before she died. It made her so happy to know I wouldn't be alone when she was gone. If she only knew how the Nightshade family has grown.

No one could deny how drastically my power grew with each lover I connected to. And from that, the power of the coven continues to grow. My grandmother used to tell me stories of her original coven in France. She had been so worried she and my mother would lose all their magic by leaving. Coming here was a tremendous risk.

I see now that this is the most powerful the Nightshade coven has been since the founding fifty years ago. And still, somehow, our strength grows each day. It makes the sun shine brighter above us and the grass grow greener beneath us. The magic surrounding our coven and our town is charged and sustained with the love I have for my men, and they for me. I feel complete with my nine. They each push me to be more than I dreamed I could be, and the coven continues to prosper.

Not to mention, at long last, I'm with child. After years of tears, worries, potions, and rituals, I will have an heir to the coven. We're unsure which of my lovers has fathered the babe, but this is the furthest along we've made it. Everyone is joyful at the announcement and eager to welcome the newest member of our coven. Especially Elias and Niall. They have such wonderful hearts. I can see them as such doting fathers. Donahue is more excited for when the child will be older and wants to play.

Even the town's human residents have offered their heartfelt congratulations.

Although, one resident hasn't been pleased. Ever since Morfran arrived in Spells Hollow two months ago, his attention has unnerved me.

He's a powerful witch, calls himself a sorcerer, and he's charming, too. Possibly the most charming man I've known. He infuriates Donahue whenever he carries my herb baskets for me. But as delightful as he seems, I have no intention of taking another lover. There's no connection with him, the way there was with my men. In fact, I sense something strange in him. A darkness. It unbalances the magic in town, around the coven I would give my life to protect.

Of course, in due time, I'll have someone else to protect.

I can't wait to start thinking of names. Adair and Peregrin say that we should wait, that we will know our child's name once they are born. However, I refuse to postpone my joy, and Verity agrees. My child will lead the coven someday, and they deserve a name that conveys the growing strength of our people. The perfect name may indeed come when I lay eyes on the babe, held fast in my arms, but I so enjoy this time of preparation.

My mother would be so proud of how far we've come. Spells Hollow is a town for all, regardless of their magical heritage. Witches and humans thrive here together in a way that could never have been possible in my grandmother's time. I owe so much to the support of my lovers and cannot wait to introduce them to their child.

The future of the Nightshade coven.

Harlow

*N**ine lovers**.*

Perhaps I didn't feel quite so bad about my current predicament.

Once again seated on the cliff side, I lay back in the grass and closed my eyes against the sun's warmth. I never spent much time outside the city as a kid, and there was a part of me that wondered what it would have been like to grow up in a coven like this. Melisande had problems here, sure, but her community was there for her. She had so much love and support from the people around her... Was that something I could have?

My head spun, the same troubles circling my mind like they were working shifts tormenting me: the quest, my family's apparent curse, Ranto and the mate bond, Kylen...

A shadow passed across my sunlight, stealing the warmth from my face before Melisande's diary was tugged from my hand.

"Hey!" I rolled to my feet and scowled at Bruin. "Give that back."

He studied the cover of the book like it held some kind of secret. Maybe the asshole didn't know how to read. Using his distraction, I surged forward, intent on retrieving it, but he simply held it above his head like a schoolyard bully.

"Come and get it."

Despite our height difference, I tried to reach his hand and achieved little more than putting a nasty smile on his face. My chest bumped into his as I pulled on his arm, pointedly ignoring the flex of his mouth-watering biceps. Losing patience, I planted both hands on his pecs and pushed. Frustration filled me when he barely took a half step back, but then his hand shot out, wrapping tightly around my throat as he pulled me into a punishing kiss.

Fuck. Him.

Ripping my mouth from his, I reared back and slapped him across the cheek. Then, like I couldn't stop myself, I gripped his jaw and drew him into a kiss that was all teeth and tongue.

Responding to my violence with the same energy, he palmed my ass and encouraged me to wrap my legs around his hips. I felt possessed. Like someone else was driving my body as I fought him for control.

"I hate you," I growled into his mouth as I rubbed against him like a bitch in heat, unable to get the leverage I needed.

"I'll see you dead, but not before I take all your pleasure. This little pussy is weeping just for me. How much does that fact make you burn?"

Without warning, he dropped my legs and carried us both down to the grass.

"I bet you won't even put up a fight while I fuck you right out here in the open. You want the others to see how you melt for the big, bad biker. How well you're going to ride my cock. Don't you, witch?"

I growled at him, desperate for him to shut up despite the way his words made my head light and my panties drenched.

"Are you going to shut the fuck up and follow through? Or

are you all talk? I'm more than happy to give your mouth something to do, although I'm sure your little biker tongue can't do to me what Ranto did last night."

At the mention of his competition, Bruin scowled, reaching for my t-shirt and whipping it over my head before I could protest. Not that I was in the mood to do more than goad him.

"I'll show you what this biker tongue can do." He lowered his head and bit my nipple through the lace of my bra, pulling off quickly with a suspicious look in his eye. Using both hands, he slid the straps off my shoulders and sucked a breath in through his teeth at the sight of my nipples, complete with titanium bars through the tip of each one.

"Fuck me," he groaned, attacking first one, then the other with his tongue.

"Kinky, but I was hoping it would be the other way around, at least for today."

"I swear to God, if I wasn't so intent on getting you on my cock, I'd gag you with it. You'd look so pretty with tears in your eyes while you silently begged me for air."

I flipped him off, and he bit down hard on my nipple in retaliation.

"Hurry up and get your pants off. Hopefully, you're big enough that I can ride you reverse cowgirl, so I don't have to look at your face."

I stripped naked as he sneered down at me before following my lead. It was a power trip to be so horrible to him, and I hated to admit that seeing his reaction was doing it for me. I rose to my knees, ready to take over the next part of the proceedings, but he flipped me back beneath him and pinned me with his hips.

"One small problem with that, Sparky. There's no way you're taking charge here." He lowered his lips until they brushed against the shell of my ear. "And when you come harder than you ever have in your life, it'll be my name on your lips and no doubt left in your mind that I'm the one inside you."

I shivered as he moved between my legs, notching his head at my entrance before he paused.

"Are you on birth control?"

I'd been on the pill for years, but it didn't stop me asking, "What if I said I wasn't?"

His grin was downright wicked as he rocked his hips, sliding his length through my arousal.

"Then it's lucky you won't live long enough to worry about motherhood."

Before I could curse him out, he thrust into me in one long stroke, and I lost all sense of reason. It was the only explanation for why I raked my fingernails down his back, letting out a scream that could have been heard from the other side of town.

Bruin set a hard pace, sliding almost all the way out before pounding into me while I hooked my heels around his ass and encouraged him to go harder.

"Is that all you've got?" I gritted between my teeth as he hit a spot so deep inside me it bordered on painful. His smirk was devastating as he lowered his head, pulling hard on my nipple piercing with his teeth.

"Fuck!" I screamed, enjoying the bite of pain as he released his hold and reached between us to rub my clit.

"I'm close, and there's no way in hell I'm going without you. Now tell me what you need to get there."

"More," I whimpered, having no clue what I meant by it. But Bruin seemed to.

He bit down on my clavicle, sucking hard. "You're wearing my mark now. Everyone will see it and know what a dirty little whore you've been for the man who is going to kill you. Your mutt will know that you may be his mate, but you'll always belong to me."

I hated the words, but my body seemed to disagree as overwhelming pleasure exploded through me. A keening cry left my lips as my back bowed, and I dug my nails deep into his shoulders to ground myself. With a deep grunt, Bruin stilled above me, his breath stuttering as he followed me into bliss. As awareness returned, I felt the itch of the grass beneath me, and the weight of a man I was supposed to hate above. A slippery stickiness slid down my leg from the place we remained joined.

What had I just done?

I'd heard of hate sex before, but this was ridiculous. And worse than the knowledge that I shouldn't have done what we just did was the sense of rightness that settled in my bones. My power buzzed contentedly beneath my skin, stronger at all the points our bodies touched, like a dog waiting for its master's attention. As my brain started to work overtime with all the new anxieties that came with hooking up with another man, Bruin's phone began to vibrate in his pocket.

"Don't you need to get that?" I didn't even care if it was his MC telling him to end me. It would give me the excuse to get away from him and process what just happened.

"Not even a little bit." His voice was muffled from where he lay half smothered in my boobs.

When he showed no sign of moving, I slid out from under him, grimacing at the mess he'd left between my thighs, and began to dress.

A small chuckle burst out of Bruin where he lay motionless on the grass, and it wasn't until I lost patience and kicked him that he slowly turned over, revealing a huge grin splitting his face. The expression startled me, seeing this always-surly guy grinning. Not smirking, not sarcastic, but genuinely amused.

"What?" I asked, fidgeting with my shirt.

"You have a hate kink."

I huffed, rolling my eyes as I finished straightening my clothing.

"No, no. I'm here for it. Honestly, it was fucking beautiful seeing you come undone like that. In fact, I can't wait to do it again."

I wanted to face palm. Maybe find a time machine and go back to tell my past self it wasn't worth the hassle. Instead, I retrieved Melisande's journal from the ground and straightened to my full height.

"That is never happening again."

His sliced eyebrow rose as I turned on my heel, heading back toward town. I pretended not to hear his parting comment. "We both know that's a lie."

It was totally a lie.

Dammit.

18

Hendrix

Coming into town was a bad idea.

I knew the witch and her growing merry band of men were still sniffing around, but everything in me screamed that the treasure I hunted was in town, and there was no way of knowing if they'd discover it first. Things could get messy when people got between a gryphon and their treasure.

The vibrations pulling at my chest took me the long way around the town, partly to keep my presence hidden from those who might exploit my ability, but mostly because... ugh. People.

I trekked along the river and came out on a grass clearing that overlooked the ocean. It would have been a lovely spot to get some sun in my gryphon form if it wasn't already occupied.

The witch—Harlow, she'd told the dog—stood toe to toe with yet another man. I couldn't make out their words, but she seemed irritated. When she slapped him for kissing her, I had a moment of confused vindication before they came together in an explosion of lust I swore I could feel from where I stood. It was raw and borderline violent, and the longer I watched, the lower my mood dropped. Still, I couldn't look away as they shed their clothes and rutted like animals out in the open for anyone to see. I pointedly ignored the fact that *I* was the *anyone* in this case.

The polite thing to do would be to leave them to it, appreciate their distraction, and continue with my hunt. Instead, I stood transfixed as her supple body moved under him. My mind conveniently overlaid the soundtrack I'd heard the night before with her current state of undress, sending bolts of arousal straight to my dick. I'd used my hand to take the edge off before, but I refused to repeat the pathetic act and turned away as the sound of her completion drifted to me on the breeze.

Without much thought to direction, except to escape the scene behind me, I barreled into the woods. The woman kept showing up. Taunting me. I raked a hand through my hair, grimacing as my fingers caught in the unruly curls. I'd thought about cutting them more times than I could count, but...well... I liked my hair. It made me feel like I could keep my mane, even in human form. The twittering of birds and a low murmur of voices nearby kept me company as I moved without purpose, trying to use momentum to puzzle out the unwelcome feelings inside of me.

"Take care, if you're heading that way."

Startled from my thoughts, I swung around to find a dirty blonde man elbow deep in moss at the base of a nearby tree.

"What?"

"About two hundred yards farther in, directly on that path, is a nasty creeper that will burn through anything it comes into contact with. My friend lost a pair of sneakers yesterday because of it. Zero out of ten, do not recommend."

"What are you...?"

A heavy hand landed on my shoulder, and I cursed my lack of attention as the dog brushed past me with a cheeky smile.

"Choose a different direction if you want to keep stomping

around. You smell stressed. And turned on. What have you been up to?" His white hair hung in long, straight sheets to his pecs. I bet he never had to deal with tangles. He didn't even seem to care about the ridiculous sequined cat t-shirt he wore.

"What are you doing here?" I asked instead of dignifying his intrusive line of questioning with an answer.

"Looking for plants with Kylen. Wanna help?"

No.

"Yes." My mouth formed the agreement before I processed what was happening, and just like that, I found myself kneeling right alongside Kylen in the dirt.

The nature witch was calm and engaging, explaining his research with a confidence I couldn't help but admire. In return, he was vocal in his interest in history, and while I wasn't about to tell him I was treasure hunting, my secondary passion was something I could lose hours talking about. I had a particular interest in supes and the crossovers between reality and fiction when it came to the myths and legends, but with the abandoned spaces of the world that I'd seen treasure hunting, I'd learned about those hidden spaces, too.

"So Atlantis?" Kylen asked, feathering his fingers through the leaves of a low-lying bush.

"Real. The whole underwater thing was a hoax, though. They had a coven of sea witches take over the government when the monarchy died and left the island destitute. Gambling debts, you know. So they raised a wall of water and used a masking spell to sink into the waves. Island gone, debt cleared, and everyone went back to business as usual. It was disappointing to find out the rumors of gold were just a myth."

Ranto snorted in his sleep, curled up at the base of a tree much like he had when he'd shared my camp the night before last, only this time he was still in human form.

I would never have admitted it out loud, but their company was...nice.

Maybe because they were both so connected to the earth that neither of them was likely to fall into the pit of empty consumerism and brainless gullibility that the masses overindulged in.

"What's the deal with the witch?"

I glanced around, hoping to find another person who had decided to speak up and ask the question that had been plaguing my mind. Nope. Apparently, it was me. Kylen glanced up with a small smirk that made me want to curse myself for showing weakness.

"Which witch?"

"Funny."

He shrugged, brushing dirt off on his ass as he straightened. "She's Harlow. We all kind of fell into this quest of hers, but between you and me, there's definitely some hinky fate thing going on here."

"There's no such thing as fate."

"Yes, there is," Ranto argued without opening his eyes.

"What would you know about it?" I'd traveled the world and never found definitive evidence of the existence of fate. Only anecdotes and starry-eyed believers whose stories seemed more serendipitous, like the discovery of penicillin, than the machinations of higher beings.

"Acts of fate guide my profession every day. An heiress's driver misses a turn and drives past her husband and his mistress on the street. A CEO's financial report file is corrupted, and he finds inconsistencies with his paperwork. A police officer asks a friend to help investigate an MC chapter, and he finds his mate along the way. Tangled webs, sure, but they always lead somewhere. You can't tell me all of these connections happen out of chaos."

That was exactly what I thought, but I'd learned a long time ago that it was useless to try to change someone's mind.

Kylen grunted beside me. "So you're investigating an MC, huh? Does that mean...?"

"Yeah, about that. If you could keep Bruin in the dark about it, I'd be in your debt. I didn't exactly mean to say that bit."

"Maybe it was fate?" I snarked.

Ranto didn't take the bait. He just let a slow smile spread across his too-perfect face.

A scream tore through the air, causing Ranto to spring to his feet as Kylen and I shared a look.

"Harlow and Bruin were hate-fucking on the cliff before. Maybe they went for round two?"

Kylen's face screwed up into a bewildered look, but before he could ask what the hell I was talking about, the sound came again.

"Okay, that was close. In town, maybe?" I said, trying to pinpoint where the noise could have come from.

Ranto and Kylen shared a look.

"Addie."

They bolted toward town, legs pumping hard as I stood alone among the trees. Whoever Addie was, it wasn't my business. I could just go back to my treasure hunt and enjoy the space the emergency would grant me. Away from everyone else.

Without making a conscious decision, I trailed after the men I'd voluntarily shared the afternoon with.

To...help?

Harlow

"*A**ddie**!*"

Panic flooded through me, and I pumped my legs harder. My lungs burned, and my calves screamed for me to slow, but that wasn't an option. I'd get to her, even if it killed me. She'd be safe. She had to be.

I'm the one who's supposed to die here. NOT HER!

Weaving between the buildings and trees, I stumbled around the corner, hitting my knee hard against the ground but forcing myself to my feet. Nothing would stop me. Another scream rang out, and I followed it to the back of the house we'd searched, hastily hopping the wooden fence and crashing into the garden.

"Addie?"

"Harlow!"

Sprinting the final few yards through the overgrown grass and plants, I skidded to a stop, throwing my arms around the teenager and squeezing hard. "I'm here. Addison, I've got you. You're okay."

"H-Harlow..." Her voice quivered, and fat tears rolled down her cheeks. "You're okay?"

I pressed my lips against the top of her head, breathing in

her cheap shampoo and reassuring myself she was alive. "Of course I'm okay, silly. It's you I was worried about."

Pulling away enough to brush her hair away from her face, I cupped her cheeks and really looked at her. Her skin was a deathly white, and she wouldn't stop crying. What the fuck had happened?

"You're alive..."

"Shh, it's okay. Let's focus on you right now."

"I saw you die!"

Neither of us moved. We could only sit there, staring into each other's eyes, both unbelievably grateful to see the other was unharmed, and yet we were terrified. Her nails dug into my forearm, clinging to me desperately as I held her face.

"They're over here," Ranto shouted as he sprinted to us from the house.

Footsteps stormed towards us, and we were swiftly surrounded by everyone asking if she was okay. Even Hendrix was here. Though he quietly remained separated from the group, his concerned eyes betrayed his composure.

"Hey! Everyone, stop talking all at once," I snapped up at them before turning my attention back to Addie. Her sobs had turned to sniffles, but she still clung to me like a lifeline. "What did you see?"

"I saw you die," she repeated, her voice cracking. "You were in front of me, yelling about a curse and someone called David? Or Donovan? I dunno. Then you started sparking the way you do when... when you think I don't see it and you let it burst outside."

A twinge pulled at my heart. I knew I wasn't hiding the sparks well, but to think she saw it when I've been at my most unstable. She could've been hurt—no, *I* could have hurt her.

"But it didn't stop. You screamed a-and..." Her words trailed off into sobs, and I held her tight. It was all I could do.

I knew this town was bad news. I'd begged her to stay home, where she was safe. This was all my fault. How was I supposed to protect her when I couldn't even look after myself?

While I panicked internally, Kylen kneeled beside us. He gently removed Addie's nails from my arm and rubbed small circles on the back of her hand with his thumb. "It's okay. Harlow's right here. We're all here for you."

She sniffled, wiping her nose with her other sleeve. "It was just so real."

"We'll figure it out," he promised her. "Can you stand?"

I mouthed a 'thank you' to him, keeping hold of Addie's other hand as we stood. Her legs wobbled, but we held her steady between us. "Wanna go inside?"

At her weak nod, we guided her towards the house. Best thing for her right now was getting away from this creepy jungle of a garden and finding her something to eat, followed by a nap. Curses could wait.

"Hold up a sec," Bruin called out, pointing at a woman in the corner of the garden. "Addie, is that who you saw?"

The fuck? I didn't see her when I jumped the fence. Actually, now that I thought about it, I hadn't seen any women in town. Just the motel.

So who the hell was she?

The woman turned, looking up at the house and... That was my face. But unlike me, she wore a modest, floor-length dress, with a flowered apron and—wait. The apron was plain.

I squinted, realizing the flowers were behind her, and I was looking *through her*.

Addie tightened her grip on my hand. "That's her."

Ranto slowly circled the translucent woman, careful not to touch her, but captivated by the resemblance. "She really does look like Harlow."

I shook my head. "No, that's not me. It's..."

"Levina Torann." Lindsay finished for me, reaching out and giving my shoulder a reassuring squeeze. "Harlow's great-something-grandmother, and from what I've read, the first victim of the Torann family's curse, after her brother."

"A ghost?" Ranto asked, rejoining the group at my side. "Can she see us?"

Hendrix shook his head. "Not likely."

Suddenly, the woman doubled over, wincing in pain as she waved her arm like she was pushing someone back.

"Get away!" she screamed, trying to back up and slipping on the grass. Sparks flew off her body wildly, her spine contorting with every bolt. *"Run while you can! This happened to Donahue. It can't be stopped!"*

"No. No, no, no, it's happening again!" Addie clung to me, her head buried in my chest with her ear pressed to my pounding heart.

I covered her other ear with my hand, unable to look away but still desperate to protect her from the screaming she was preparing for.

"It's too late for me, but you must save yourselves," Levina begged through her tears. *"Find a way to break it. Don't let the curse take you and the children! Now RUN!"*

The lightning came faster, firing off her in every direction as she writhed in the grass. She tried to curl up from the pain, but she was no longer in control of her body. All she could do was scream until the lightning hit her too frequently to take a breath between strikes.

In one final movement, Levina whipped up to her knees, mouth open in a silent, breathless scream, as her entire body was enveloped in electricity. It lit up the garden in a bright light, forcing us to look away.

By the time the light dissipated, Levina was simply gone.

"So, that's what death by curse looks like..." I muttered, thinking back to the family tree. Every death in over three centuries, leading straight down to me.

"Is it over?" Addie squeaked.

"Yeah, I think so. Let's get inside," I said, reluctantly loosening my grip on her.

"What the fuck was that shit?" Bruin growled, his eyes wide as Lindsay pushed past him, guiding Addie's shaking form inside before the ghost could reappear.

"Seriously? Don't you know anything?" Hendrix pushed off his spot against the wall, rolling his eyes.

"Sorry, looks like I skipped my ghost-busting classes in high school."

"It was a death loop. And a pretty bad one at that. It's something that happens to ghosts with significant trauma. They get stuck, constantly reliving a moment of pain and confusion."

Bruin scoffed. "Yeah, I'd say dying like that would be pretty fucking traumatic."

His eyes narrowed on me, and I avoided his gaze. As I looked around, everyone was staring at me. "Something on my face?"

"More like your face on someone else, Sparky."

Kylen stepped between us, blocking the jerk from my sight. "Lindsay said you're related?"

I shifted on my feet, the itch to burn off some energy quickly rising. "Yep. That was three hundred-year-old Gram-Gram-Levina. Never sent any birthday cards, but you can't deny her skill at traumatizing teenagers."

Kylen didn't rise to my comments, "What did he mean when he said the Torann family curse?"

"I think we all just saw what he meant."

"So that's going to happen to—"

"Stop it. I'm done with this conversation."

Spinning on my heel, I took the stairs two at a time to get back in the house, no Addie or Lindsay in sight. Good. The farther they got from here, away from me, the better.

"Harlow," Ranto called after me.

I was barely two steps inside when he pulled me back. The familiar, soothing buzz in my chest urged me to dive into his arms, but I couldn't. Not after what we'd just seen.

"No!" I snapped, lunging out of arm's reach before turning back to him, then away... I didn't know what to do.

My head spun as electricity crackled against my knuckles. I needed to punch something. I wanted to cry. To scream. To be held, and fucked, and loved, before it was too late. I'd seen my fate, and any moment now, Levina's death would begin its loop again. She would continue to repeat her most painful moment for eternity, and soon it really would be me dying in front of everyone.

Shaking the sparks off my hands, I made my decision. At least, for now.

"Leave me alone."

I ran.

September 7th, 1672.

It pains me to admit it, but I admire Morfran's tenacity. I've never known someone to persist in courting an uninterested woman for over a decade, yet here he remains.

It's never ending. The stares when he thinks I don't see him in the corner of a room. The anonymous gifts left on the porch at least thrice per month. The lingering touches too intimate for a mere greeting. I see each as a warning.

He tells me he worships me the way sailors do the sun after a storm. He even started calling me that a few years ago; the town's sun. A brightness shining down upon the coven. Providing warmth, hope, and life to the land. An entity shining so brightly, no night could ever last forever upon the earth.

Well, if I am the sun, he is a shadow, threatening to eclipse me from my people and leave Spells Hollow in eternal darkness. He does not worship me. He obsesses over the power I hold, the magic I share between my lovers, and yearns for it.

I've rejected his proposals time after time. It isn't a matter of my refusal to take another lover. In fact, if I met someone with whom I shared the same connection as my others, I would accept them immediately. However, Morfran and I don't share the connection he believes we do. He uses his magic recklessly, with no thought to the balance of the land. Over the years, his power has become rooted in something sinister.

My grandmother created Spells Hollow as a sanctuary for magic and those who wield it, and I have upheld the tradition by allowing Morfran to live with us. However, I had to deny him access to the Nightshade coven for fear of his magic spreading its darkness throughout. He's lived with these restrictions quietly, but I've sensed how dangerous he's become over the years.

It is not the rituals of the coven he seeks; he's never been interested in being part of that side of the community in any capacity greater than he is now. What he desires is the power in leading the coven. The things he has said about the colonies growing over this new land lead me to believe he sees my people as an army. He admonishes my men for not doing more outside of our town, but that is not where our concern lies.

The way he looks at my children, the future of this coven, leaves me fearful. His stare is both covetous and full of revulsion. I do not know whether he dreams of being their father or destroying them entirely. Both thoughts make me sick.

We've already begun training my eldest to inherit my position someday. I thought it prudent to start much earlier than my own training did, in case something should happen. Donahue believes I worry for nothing, that he and the others would ensure I live long beyond my mother. It is not that I doubt him. I simply need the reassurance that the magic of this coven will live on without me.

But as the days go on, my fears only grow. Morfran's actions consistently become more erratic, and I know there will soon be a breaking point. For now, I can only continue to prepare for that day.

I am no sun. Nightshade witches are born of the blood moon, and to protect my town, I am not afraid to feed the moon as much blood as it desires.

Those who would do us harm, beware.

Harlow

"What kind of comfort read is this?" I groused, still feeling out of sorts from the vivid image of my own death that wasn't actually mine. Was that what I'd look like when the curse took me?

The way her power had torn her apart before...

I shuddered, shifting back from the edge of the cliff to stand. This little overlook had fast become my favorite place to take a time out, to learn more about the coven and hopefully figure out how the hell to avoid dying.

I shook my hands out, ignoring the snap and crackle of energy that sparked from my fingers with the movement. I was in control. No rogue powers here. I wished I believed it.

My stomach turned, and even the cool sea breeze did nothing to soothe my stress-heated skin. Had she exploded? Or had it been more of an implosion? I felt like it was an important distinction, because if I was a hazard to Addie or Lindsay when the curse detonated me, I didn't want them caught in the fallout.

Was it hot out here?

I flapped my tank top, trying to create a breeze as my chest tightened. Hoo-wee, it was getting a little difficult to breathe.

Okay, hands on knees and just focus on the in and out. In through the nose, and out through the mouth. In through the...

I cut off mid-panic as a sharp cry echoed through the air.

"What the hell is that?"

The creature had wings bigger than any bird I'd ever seen, which was a good thing because the lion-type body seemed to defy all laws of aerodynamics. I mean... they were the same laws that said bumble bees shouldn't have been able to fly, so I guess this was another strike against science.

The lion-bird skimmed the tree line, heading deeper into the woods and, without giving it much thought, I followed. Luckily—or perhaps unluckily, depending on how receptive the beast was to company—it didn't seem to have a stealth mode, and the size made it easy to follow from the ground. I tripped over tree roots and stumbled through low-lying bushes, keeping one eye on the gaps in the branches so I didn't lose sight of it.

After a time, I came out into a familiar grass clearing and slowed to a stop as the creature landed on the far side of a cold fire pit. Its feathered head swung toward me, studying me with a beady bird eye.

"Hi. Nice bird-lion thing. You're friendly, right? I probably should have worked that out before following you out into the middle of nowhere." My mouth kept running while inwardly I cringed. I hadn't had this bad of a case of verbal diarrhea since...

The beast reared on its hind legs, and I took a quick step back, preparing to run. It stretched its wings wide as its shape shimmered into a slimmer humanoid... Hendrix.

The beast was Hendrix.

"Did you just call me a lion-bird? The word you want is gryphon, you heathen." His words were as grumpy as the last couple of times I'd met him, but this time there was an odd curl to his lip. Like he was amused by my ignorant ass rather than offended.

I suppressed an answering smile, flipping my hand while I tried to play off the mistake. "Well, I mean, you're half bird, half lion. What was I supposed to think?"

He crossed the clearing, closing in until we were almost toe to toe. Ducking his head to look me in the eye, he pointed at himself. "Gryphon."

"Gryphon," I repeated, enjoying the happy buzz my power gave me being so close to him.

The reminder of my powers was like a bucket of ice water, wiping my mind clear of the gryphon distraction and right back to the panic attack.

"Whoa, where did you go?" he asked, gripping my shoulders as the clearing went for a spin.

"I just..." I looked up into his warm eyes and wished, for a moment, that things could be heading in a different direction.

"I'm going to die. Probably soon. Definitely, probably in some kind of a full body meltdown like that death loop we saw before. That's going to be me, and Addie and Lindsay are going to see it. I don't know how to stop it." He held me upright as I said the words I'd been hiding from since this whole quest had started.

"My powers are unstable, and I'm scared I'll lose control."

I had never admitted to being afraid in my life.

The uncomfortable awareness of my vulnerability crawled through my body, battering against the fear and anxiety until I worried it would all bubble out of me in some toxic, emotional vomit.

"What do you need?" Hendrix's fingers tapped out a nervous rhythm on my shoulders, clearly as far out of his comfort zone as I felt. I had only met him in passing a couple of times. Had never been alone with him. And yet, the answer that fell from my lips didn't catch me by surprise the way it did him.

"You."

His jaw dropped, and I hesitated, wondering if I should just hope for the earth to open up and swallow me whole. My vagina and I really needed to have a chat. The problem was, the more I read about Melisande's men, the more it felt right to pursue the impulses I felt around certain new friends.

Even Bruin. Dammit.

As we stood in silence, my plea hanging in the air, Hendrix's face went through an array of emotions. Shock, confusion, a brief glimpse of something not so nice, and then he cocked his head, brow furrowed as though he were trying to solve a complex puzzle.

When I couldn't stand the silence any longer, I stepped back out of his grip, an apology perched on my tongue.

The movement seemed to snap him out of whatever was going on for him, though, because my "sorry" was interrupted by his "take what you need from me."

We both froze.

My palms started to sweat as I huffed a small laugh. Why did he make me feel so awkward? Sure, he was crazy hot, but so were Ranto, Bruin, Kylen... damn. My libido was turned up to one hundred.

"I shouldn't have... I mean... really?"

He dipped his chin, reaching for my hand. Ugh. Sweaty hands. I subtly wiped them on my shorts before accepting his offer and let him lead the way over to his tent. This was really happening. As we passed through the campsite, visions of my time with Ranto flashed through my mind, adding to the nerves that squirmed in my belly.

"Can I touch you?" I blurted.

He paused, one hand on the tent flap.

"You want to touch me?"

"Yes."

He waved me inside, and I hurriedly dropped to my knees to crawl in. There wasn't much room to move once the outside world was shut out, but I couldn't bring myself to care as he joined me, sitting back on his heels so his head wouldn't brush the roof. I reached across the space between us, hand hovering just above his chest as I waited for his reaction.

"Take what you need from me," he repeated, wrapping a large hand around mine and pressing it to him firmly.

At first contact, I knew I needed more. With very little finesse, I reached for the hem of his shirt, shamelessly stripping it from his body so I could press my hands to his skin. He shivered under my touch, emboldening me to explore further. Lower. I tilted my chin up, silently asking for his lips as my fingers brushed against the waist of his jeans.

The first brush of his mouth against mine was a barely there tease that set us both alight. With a groan, his arms wrapped around me as he speared his tongue past my lips, licking and sucking in a way that left me feeling thoroughly owned. Not to be outdone, I pushed him onto his back and straddled his hips before diving back into the kiss. His hips rocked up into me, and I gasped at the friction, still a little sore from my time with Bruin on the cliffs. But right now, all I wanted was more of Hendrix. I needed to feel closer to him.

"I want to taste you."

I'd been thinking of it since Ranto outed him the night before. The idea that our noises could get him worked up to the point of release made my pussy weep. I kissed down his torso, nipping at his skin as my hands made quick work of his button and zipper.

"Yes," he hissed as I dipped a hand into his underwear and wrapped my fingers around his length. The swollen, purple head disappeared beneath my fist as I pumped him slowly, watching his eyes cloud with lust.

"Is this what you did when you heard me with Ranto yesterday?" I asked.

His hips jerked, unable to get far underneath my weight. Shifting off him, I got comfortable on my belly and dragged my tongue up the underside of his cock. The bitter, salty taste of precum hit my mouth, and I sucked gently on the plum-shaped head.

"Is this what you imagined while he made me cum?"

He nodded. "Yesterday. And today."

"Naughty boy. Were you watching me with Bruin?"

He studied me through hooded eyes, chest heaving. I wondered where he'd watched us from. Had he enjoyed it? The thought of him watching us from the shadows sent a jolt of arousal through me, and I squeezed my thighs together.

"Did you like watching him fuck me?"

"Yes." The word hissed through his teeth, and I rewarded him by swallowing his cock.

Pressing hard with my tongue and giving just the hint of a scrape with my teeth, I worked him hard, relishing the grunts and moans that escaped his sinful mouth. I may be a blathering mess around him ninety-nine percent of the time, but I'd always been confident in the bedroom. Making my partner feel good satisfied me almost as much as a good orgasm.

When I glanced toward his face again, he was half sitting up, eyes fixed on where my lips stretched around his impressive girth. I popped off and gave him a cheeky grin before diving back down, relishing the rough curse that fell from him. A few moments later, his breathing changed, and he cupped my jaw gently in his firm hand.

"I'm about to come."

I didn't want to stop. I wanted to feel him come apart under me. To swallow him down and accept all he'd give me. Squeezing his hand in acknowledgement, I doubled down, concentrating on his tip while I worked his length with my fist.

"Fuck, you're perfect."

His grip tightened on me, and I felt the pulse under my tongue before his release filled my mouth. I swallowed fast, only gagging a little as his orgasm stretched on longer than expected. Eventually, he flopped back against the ground, and I crawled up his body to snuggle into his side.

"That was..." I tried to find a word to describe how much I'd enjoyed what we'd done.

When he didn't reply, I waited in the silence, hoping I hadn't epically screwed up somehow.

Why wasn't he talking?

Maybe I'd read the room wrong, and he was trying to figure out how to tell me to leave. The thought didn't sit well, but when I pulled back, the conflict was there on his face.

Well, this is awkward.

I had more dignity than to become the clingy girl who didn't read the room after sex, so instead of having the talk, I gathered my courage and prepared to leave.

Hey, at least he'd taken my mind off the whole dying thing for a little while.

"Where are you going?"

"I was... ah... I don't... Where are you going?" Well done, Harlow. Idiot.

Hendrix slid a hand beneath his head, and I dug my nails into my palms to keep from drooling at the flex of his bicep.

"Do you know why I'm in Spells Hollow?"

I eased myself into a seated position and cocked my head, wondering where he was going with the question.

"How would I know when you haven't told me?"

He grunted, as though I should have just known. Seriously, the guy was confusing as hell sometimes.

"I forgot you don't know about my kind."

"Lion-birds?" I joked.

"Gryphons." He pulled me back down beside him and flicked my nose. "I'm a treasure hunter. My kind excel at finding and hoarding things of value."

"Like dragons?"

He snorted.

"Stop interrupting. Especially with insulting comparisons like that. Now. I came to Spells Hollow because I had the sense a great treasure was here. Something life-changing. Something I had to have."

I nodded, scowling as I thought it through. I'd been around a lot of Spells Hollow in the past few days, and while the town was rich in history, I hadn't seen anything of significant monetary value.

"Do you think it's in one of the houses we can't get into? We can help you, if you want, but I'm pretty sure Bruin will try to take it from you. Maybe we should keep it a secret."

His chuckle rumbled through me.

"Thank you for the offer, but I'm pretty sure I've found it. Not quite what I was expecting, but I can't say that I'm disappointed."

"What?"

"You."

Oh. Ohhhhh. "I think that's the corniest thing I've ever heard."

He palmed my face and pushed as he rolled out from under me. Grabbing his shirt, he re-dressed while I pouted at him covering up all the delicious muscles.

"Aaaand you ruined it. Come on, Treasure, give me a minute to pack up camp, then I'll walk you back to town."

Bruin

Where the fuck had they stashed my bike? If someone had stolen it—ignoring the fact it was made from stolen parts in the first place—while I was stuck on this job, I was gonna be pissed. I'd already searched all around the gas station and the diner. The only place left was the woods behind the motel, and I'd been avoiding that since a deceptively kind waitress at the diner had told me it was perfectly safe. I'd stopped believing that bitch after she told me the apple pie was fresh out of the oven and it arrived stale as fuck.

You don't mess with a man's pie like that.

Creeping into the woods, I walked parallel to the motel, one line of trees deep. I doubted Lindsay would've gone in much farther alone. Just far enough so the bike wouldn't be immediately visible from the motel.

As I meandered between the trees, my phone vibrated in my pocket. Ah, fuck. I'd ignored the last three calls.

Let's get this over with.

"You know, Sandra's gonna get jealous if you keep calling me like this."

Kevin snarled into the phone, forcing me to hold it away

from my ear. "How fucking long does it take to put a bullet in someone's head?"

I waited a moment to make sure he was done with his temper tantrum, before bringing the phone back to my ear. "Well, you know me. I thought I'd take my time. See the sights, absorb the history of the town and all that. There's some fascinating stuff here."

"Oh, yeah? Like some bitch's magic cunt?"

My moment of surprised silence was enough for him.

"Thought so." He chuckled, and the sound made my fist clench and fantasies about ramming it through his skull danced through my head. "Going soft, brother? Got some new loyalties?"

"Never," I growled through gritted teeth.

"Good. Now that's cleared up, lemme make this nice and easy for you. You deliver her body, or I'll come with the boys to collect it myself. And while I'm visiting Spells Hollow, I'll have my old Enforcer dealt with. See, he's always been sore he didn't get my patch and—"

"You done listening to yourself talk?" I snapped. "Fucking relax, Kev. I'll bring you the body on time, like I've always done."

"You better, or else I'll—"

I tapped my phone and immediately turned it off, ending the call before he could hit me with a well-rehearsed threat that would obviously leave me shaking in my boots. Idiot. I was the only reason he hadn't lost his position years ago, and he thought he could try to threaten me? Fucking cute.

It left me in an awkward position, though. He wanted Harlow dead, and I...

"I really thought you'd be more observant of someone following you."

Despite nearly shitting my heart outta my dick, I held onto my composure as I turned around to see Kylen leaning against a tree, arms folded across his chest. Fuck. How much had he heard?

"Aww, did you miss me?"

"Apparently not as much as your boss."

Double fuck.

"Kev?" I scoffed. "He's a pushover. Shoulda seen when Harlow took him out. She didn't even need to use her magic."

"So that's why he's using you to kill her?"

Goddamn it! I don't need this right now.

"Why don't we talk about something else?"

"No, I wanna know." He narrowed his eyes, pushing off the tree to square up against me. "Are you seriously still going to kill her, after everything you've seen here? After you *fucked her*?"

"Ooh, someone's jealous. Was your little kiss not enough?" I grinned, leaning closer. His addictive pine and soil scent filled my nostrils as I whispered in his ear. "Want me to tell you how she screamed for me? How she felt around my dick when she came."

Kylen's back stiffened at my words, our chests brushing against each other as he shuddered out a breath.

"Or better question..." I mused, my voice low and seductive. "Why do you want me to try to kill her? Do you miss wrapping me up in vines like a present? They didn't exactly hide your attraction to me."

"Is that what you think?" he asked, turning his head to face me.

Our breath mingled between us as I stared through his glasses into bright blue eyes. I could even see a little yellow in them, right around the pupil. Fuck, he was so pretty. It wouldn't take any effort at all to close the gap between our mouths. His full, pink lips were practically begging me to kiss him.

"I think you followed me out here because you were hoping for something to happen." I snaked my arms around his hips, hooking my fingers into his belt loops to pull him closer. "Mm, feels like I was right."

His hard length pressed against my own, and his eyelashes fluttered in response to the sensation. Fucking *beautiful.* Unable to resist, I dragged my tongue along the curve of his jaw, gently tugging his earlobe between my teeth.

"Bruin." His gasp was music to my ears, and I needed to hear it again. Both of his hands cupped my jaw as he maneuvered me back in front of his face. "Are you sure about this?"

I nodded, practically drooling from my hunger for him. "Definitely."

Before I could check he was okay, too, he crushed his mouth to mine, immediately meeting my tongue in a battle for dominance that neither of us truly cared to win. The fight was far more fun.

Our push and pull of desperate kisses soon had me backed up against a tree. I ran my hands over the tight cheeks of Kylen's fucking stunning ass. His hips ground against my own, and I held him there, bucking up into the delicious friction between our bodies.

"Take off your shirt. Now," he ordered, pulling away enough to tug his own over his head.

Holy crap, who'd have thought the botanist would have abs?

Grinning at my luck, I threw off my shirt and reached out to run my hands over those muscles, but had my arms pulled up above my head. Were those...

"You were right earlier," he explained. "I really do miss the sight of you tied up and desperate."

Vines. Hello, old friends.

Kylen licked and sucked down the pulse in my neck as his vines securely pinned me against the tree. The bark dug into my back painfully, but the pleasure coming from my front far outweighed it.

"You better not be just teasing me." I chuckled, only half-joking.

His hands smoothed across my waistband, fingertips dipping below the clothing, and he whispered in my ear. "It's not a tease if you fully intend to go through with it."

Our lips met again as Kylen ran his hands back up my chest to rub and pinch at my nipples. I moaned into his mouth, desperately needing to get out of my pants before I ruined them. Unfortunately for me, Kylen only smirked against my lips, practically preening at the sounds escaping me, then reached around to grip my ass tight.

I'd never been this turned on by a man touching me like this. Usually, I was the one in control, leading the dance and taking what I needed from my partner. But with Kylen, I needed him to touch me however he desired. I wanted to be at his mercy. And fuck, I'd probably cum in my pants if he called me his good boy again.

"Huh, what's this?" Feeling a lump in my back pocket, he reached in and pulled out a small bottle of lube, raising one eyebrow. "And you said I was the one who came out here with expectations?"

I shrugged as much as I could with my arms pinned above me. "To be honest, I was also hoping Harlow would be up for anal at some point. Boy Scouts taught me to always be prepared."

"No way were you a boy scout."

"Sure was. You should see my rope skills." I grinned wider, and his vines tightened, pulling me up on my tiptoes.

"I think mine are better."

"No arguments here."

With another pinch to my nipple, Kylen licked and nibbled at the other while stroking over my abs, steadily moving down to my waistband. He quickly removed my belt and unbuttoned my jeans, dragging them down as he dropped to his knees and palmed the tent in my briefs. Looking up at me with wide, blue eyes, he slowly licked the thin fabric.

I groaned low in my throat, positive there were at least two wet spots on my briefs now. As he tugged my underwear down my thighs and freed my aching cock, he smirked and sucked the head into his mouth, swirling his tongue around it like it was the best treat he'd ever tasted. I closed my eyes, hips twitching, but he wouldn't take in any more of me. I craved more of his mouth's heat, but as I dangled from the tree, my toes only just touching the ground, I couldn't get the leverage to thrust between his lips. He had me completely at his mercy, and I loved it.

He pulled back and breathed over my length. "Want more?"

"Yes. Gods, yes."

"You're a witch. What's the magic word?"

I chuckled, probably closer to a desperate giggle. "Please, Kylen. Please suck me."

"Good boy."

In a total U-turn from his earlier movements, Kylen dove onto my cock, sucking me into the back of his throat until he gagged. The sudden pleasure knocked the breath out of me, and I wheezed, looking down to watch him bob his head on my length, gagging every time I hit his throat and pressing down on his own crotch with the heel of his hand.

Holy shit, he loves choking on my cock.

Summoning the scraps of my strength, I looped one leg over his shoulder and pulled him in so his nose pressed right against my pelvis. His throat constricted around me, and tears welled in his eyes, but he stayed there, staring up at me for long seconds before he tapped my thigh twice. I quickly let him up for air, mesmerized by the scarlet flush of his cheeks and the string of drool connecting his lips to the wet tip of my dick.

He smirked, wiping away the drool. "Brat."

"Eh, I've been called worse."

"I don't doubt it." He flicked the cap on the lube he stole from me and squirted his fingers.

"Y'know, I think my dick's already plenty wet with your spit if you wanna finish me off with a hand."

He grinned wickedly. Shit, I didn't know he could do that. He was supposed to be the good one.

"You're right, but I have a better idea." The vines twisted above me, spinning me until I faced the tree, then I felt a slick finger between my cheeks. "Tell me, has anyone ever had you here, Bruin?"

"Mm, fuck, you'd be the first."

His finger pressed against my hole, circling it as he leaned around my hip to lick the bead of precum from the head of my cock. As my hole twitched under his ministrations, he steadily eased his slick fingertip in and out of me. It was the most gentle tease of what was to come, and I felt sure he'd drive me mad if he kept going at this frustratingly slow pace.

Inch by inch, he slowly worked his finger inside until I was panting. I didn't hear him move, but the next thing I knew stood behind me, whispering in my ear like I'd done to him earlier. "You're so tight. Do you think you can handle another?"

"If you don't start fucking me in the next minute, I'm going to suffocate you on my dick the next time it's anywhere near your mouth."

In response, he added another finger and started stretching me for real. He kissed up and down my neck, soothing the burn as he mused, "Let's give it four minutes. I don't wanna hurt your virgin hole."

"Kylen—"

As I raised my voice to tell him what I really thought of him, he slapped his free hand over my mouth. "Shh, you don't want anyone hearing you, do you? We're only yards from the motel, and I don't think you want the others to literally catch you with your pants around your ankles."

He chuckled while he moved his fingers inside me, finally brushing over my prostate and making me see stars. I moaned into his hand, and he did it again.

"You're a noisy slut, aren't you?"

Removing his hands and his fingers, the heat of his body left my back, and I struggled to catch my breath. This man would be the death of me.

"Here. Open wide," he sang in a whisper, then stuffed black fabric into my mouth that smelled awfully familiar. My shirt, the bastard.

While I let out a string of muffled curses, the vines slowly lowered me to the ground, enough that I could bend my knees a little. But before I could enjoy my new range of movement, more plantlife snaked up my ankles, their strength spreading my legs and preventing further movement. Fucking wonderful.

Kylen's hands gripped my hips, pulling me back to feel his hot, slicked length grind along my crack. "Remember," he whispered, "You wanted to be impatient. This might pinch."

His cock brushed against my entrance again, only this time, the mushroom head started to push inside.

Holy fuck, that was more than a pinch.

I bore down on the intrusion, biting the shirt in my mouth as his cock slid into me a little farther with each thrust until finally his hips were flush with my ass.

Kylen whispered in my ear, "I'm all the way inside. That's my good boy. Are you ready?"

I nodded, preening at the pet name I'd absolutely deny later. But right now, I just needed him to pound me into next week.

Gripping my hips hard enough I thought they might bruise, Kylen started to fuck me in earnest. Despite his want for quiet in case we were heard, the smacking of our joining echoed in the forest, but neither of us could bring ourselves to care.

"You're taking me so well," he praised. "Oh, just look at your hole stretched around me, so fucking full of my cock. That's it. You're so good, baby."

His words went straight to my weeping dick, and I whimpered. Fuck, I'd never whimpered before in my life, but this man had an effect on me that defied science. It was pure magic.

He picked up the pace, slamming our hips together at a brutal pace, his cock hitting my prostate dead on every time. I couldn't even move enough to meet his thrusts. All I could do was let my eyes roll back, moan into my shirt, and take what he gave. And oh boy, was he a giver.

"Are you gonna cum? Look at you, I bet I don't even need to touch your cock. You'll cum just by bouncing on my dick, my needy little slut."

My inner muscles contracted, and my cock jerked violently, painting the tree with long spurts of my cum. Lucky for me, I was held in place by vines, or I would've fallen face-first onto my own release. Kylen's thrusts stuttered as he watched, then quickly followed me, groaning into my ear.

If I hadn't just come, that sound would've gotten me instantly hard.

We stood there for a few minutes, panting against each other, cum running down my leg, until I wiggled my shoulders a little. Still unable to speak, I moaned around my shirt again, hoping he'd take the hint.

"Huh? Oh yeah, shit, sorry."

The vines around my arms and ankles retracted, and Kylen helped me stand by myself for the first time in way too long. Once I pulled my shirt out of my mouth, I grabbed Kylen's face for a filthy kiss that was all tongue.

I grinned against his lips. "We're definitely doing that again."

We dressed quickly and wobbled back to the motel, satisfied grins plastered across our faces, only to bump into Harlow and Hendrix walking up from the Spells Hollow road. Ranto had briefly introduced him after the exploding ghost thing. Apparently, he was a cool guy, but I'd see about that.

"Oh, hey." Harlow waved, and my eyes narrowed on her other hand, linked with Hendrix's.

Welcome to the club, buddy.

"Where've you guys been?"

Kylen answered before I could get awkward. "Looking for the big guy's bike. I'm thinking we just get Lindsay to give it back."

"You think?"

He looked at me, a smile curling the corner of his mouth. "He's not going anywhere."

We headed into the motel only for Lindsay to immediately usher us away from Addie and Ranto. He gently closed the connecting door and turned to us.

"Sorry about that. She finally fell asleep, and I don't wanna wake her. And obviously Ranto is joining nap time." He looked us over, eyes narrowing in suspicion. “Hm, you two seem extra close.”

“We found some common ground.” I grinned. “I think Harlow and the new guy did, too.”

Lindsay whipped his head around to his bestie, completely forgetting about us. “Another one?”

Harlow shrugged, still not letting go of his hand. “What can I say? Stuff happened. He calls me his treasure.”

“That’s so sweet I’d gag if I still had the reflex.”

Harlow

CONSIDERING the death sentence hanging over my head, the next few days passed in relative peace.

I was… happy.

Hendrix, the traitor, ratted me out for my mini freak out, and Kylen proposed we work on some grounding exercises to help when I felt overwhelmed by my power. I wasn't sure it would help, but I couldn't argue the point when he reminded me of how he and Ranto had helped me calm the energy before.

Ranto, who had been watching people walk past outside, had volunteered to help.

Bruin continued to be a pain in my ass at every opportunity, but where before I took his death threats seriously, the last few days, he'd made it seem more like foreplay.

I never claimed we weren't fucked up. Sue me.

Despite the happy news that Hendrix had found Ranto's bag in the woods, he continued to wear Lindsay's gaudy clothing. I smiled at the bright yellow sleeveless hoodie he'd picked out for the day. His shoulders bulged in a way that made me shift in my seat every time I saw him move. It would have been impossible to resist him if it weren't for the Pikachu ears sticking up from the top of the hood. His beautiful white hair was neatly tucked away, and I wondered if he'd agree to take it off while we trained.

"Are you listening?" Kylen asked, drawing my attention to where he crouched in the grass beside the gallows. Bruin and Hendrix had taken a seat on the wooden monstrosity to watch.

"Ahhh..."

"You're staring at his arms." He waved a hand at the arms I had very much been watching closely.

"Do you blame me?"

"No. But you can play later. Now it's time to work."

I sighed and closed my eyes, focusing on the power inside me.

"Now, let it out. Just a little."

"That's what she said."

I opened my eyes to glare at Bruin. Unconvinced by the innocent look he sent me.

"Ignore him. Feel it build deep in your core until you're overflowing with it."

A loud snort behind me broke my concentration again. Hendrix pointed at Bruin.

"Oh, come on. That was you!"

"Can you both shut it, please?" Kylen snapped, scowling at them until they held their hands up in surrender.

"Okay. Let it build until you're ready to explode, and then—"

"Come your brains out?" Hendrix asked.

I flinched at the sharp crack of the two idiots behind me high fiving. Ladies and gentlemen, the men I'd decided to sleep with.

Kylen huffed, glancing over his shoulder. His posture screamed his desire to disappear into the woods with his plants. I cupped his elbow, keeping him in place while hoping he could read how much I appreciated him.

"Oh, come on. You're making it too easy," Bruin whined.

"One more word out of either of you, and I'll use you for target practice," I growled, shooting Kylen a small smile. He nodded, and we repositioned ourselves to try again.

Okay. I could do this. Deep breath in, long breath out. Focus the energy in my center...

A loud cough pulled my attention away just as I let go of the energy, and a bolt of lightning streaked toward the gallows. Hendrix and Bruin dove toward the ground just as the wooden structure caught the energy and absorbed it.

Huh.

No wonder the thing had stood for hundreds of years.

Hendrix pushed to his feet, throwing me an apologetic look while Bruin took his time getting off the ground.

"You did that on purpose."

"Nope, but I can if you want me to." I smirked.

"I think we need to try a new approach," Kylen muttered, rubbing his forehead. "Has it occurred to anyone that this could be what we need to do to break the curse? We saw Harlow's ancestor doppelganger basically vaporize herself when she lost control of her powers. It seems like it might be a good idea to start there with saving her life. Think about it. We all ended up here at the same time. All our powers complement each other. Air, electricity, weather, nature. All of them. It has to be fate."

"There's no such thing as fate," Hendrix muttered.

"Still sticking to that belief even after you found your treasure?" Ranto asked, the challenge clear in his tone.

"Let's just take a break. I need some air."

Before anyone else could jump in to argue, I left them to it. It had been days since we had witnessed the death loop, and I still couldn't talk or think about what had happened. I wasn't at panic-attack levels of distress anymore, but the reality that I might have witnessed what fate, or whatever, had in store for me was a little too close for comfort.

Despite my claim, I found myself drawn toward my ancestor's home. Hurrying through the front door to avoid looking at the gardens for fear of seeing the death loop reappear, I took the stairs to the second floor and stalled out in one of the bedrooms. By the silver mirror and glass vials lined up along a vanity table in the corner, I guessed I'd found Levina's room. A layer of dust coated the contents of the room, and I wondered if they had cast cleaning spells back when there was a family in residence. It seemed like the kind of thing families would have done. Picking up one of the old vials, I caught the faintest whiff of lavender. Perhaps Levina had sleep troubles? I eyed her bed, then, following an impulse I didn't understand, stripped off the heavy, dusty covers and lay down on the mattress.

Had she known about the curse? I wondered if she had lain in this spot and contemplated her fate like I was now. Or maybe avoidance was a family trait, and she'd ignored the problem. An even worse thought occurred to me. What if she'd thought she could break it, too? Maybe I was destined to go out in a surge of energy regardless of what I did.

"You're thinking pretty hard in there, Treasure."

I rolled my head to the side to find Hendrix leaning in the doorway with Ranto right behind him. With a sigh, I sat up and craned my neck to see if anyone else had ignored my need for space.

"Kylen took Lindsay and Addie into the woods to play in the dirt, and Bruin is off somewhere being Bruin. It's just us."

"What are you guys doing here?"

His lip ticked up in a small smile as he crossed the room uninvited and sat beside me on the bed. Ranto followed him in and leaned his hip against Levina's vanity table.

"Can you please take off the Pikachu vest? It's really hard to take you seriously in it," I moaned, my hormones confused about whether we were turned on by his sculpted arms while the damn ears bobbed on his hood. He flashed me a wicked grin and reached for the hem.

"If you insist." He removed the fabric with a flourish, revealing a long, lean torso with defined six pack and divots over his hips that I suddenly wanted to trace with my tongue more than anything.

Whelp, that cleared things up. We were most definitely turned on.

"Keep looking at me like that, mate, and we're going to need some privacy."

"Oh, hell no. I'm not going anywhere." Hendrix shifted closer to me on the bed.

I shot him a smug look, thinking of our conversation and wondering whether he was intent on voyeurism... or joining. A shiver of delight worked its way over my shoulders, and I realized either way I'd enjoy the hell out of the next little while.

Ranto shrugged. "As long as Harlow doesn't mind, it's fine with me. As long as you're okay with sharing."

I raised my hand as though we were sitting in a classroom.

"I, for one, am very okay with sharing."

Ranto chuckled but made no move to cross the room. I arched a brow at him, hoping he'd close the distance, but his smile only grew.

"I think we'd better start by getting our mate naked. Wouldn't you say, gryphon?"

Hendrix hummed low in his throat as he shifted to press his front to my back. His hands squeezed my shoulders, then slid down my arms until he reached the hem of my t-shirt. Running his hands up my sides, he pushed the fabric up and encouraged me to lift my arms while I panted at the sensations his touch evoked in my body. We'd barely started, and I was already so wet I worried I'd leave a stain on the mattress. Sorry great-, great-, whatever grandmother. If she was anything like Melisande, maybe she'd be impressed that the bed was seeing action again after all these years.

I was keeping them both, I decided as my bra was removed and Ranto's eyes darkened at the sight of my piercings.

"Damn, girl."

Without an ounce of shame, he reached down and adjusted the impressive tent in his sweats. I licked my lips, tracking the movement as Hendrix reached around and tweaked my nipples.

"Please," I whimpered, unsure what I wanted, but unwilling to wait for it.

"Pants," Ranto ordered, his eyes locked on Hendrix's hand as it slipped down my front to tease the waistband.

Why hadn't I worn a skirt? Except for the fact I didn't own one, the easy access would have been super handy right now. Strong hands grasped my hips and encouraged me up off the bed, and rather than waiting for the slow undressing, I decided to take matters into my own hands. In one quick move, I pushed my pants and panties to the floor, bending at the waist to give Hendrix a show. What I hadn't expected was for him to palm my ass cheeks and lick me from clit to asshole.

"Shit!" I squeaked, almost losing my balance as he took another, slower lick.

"Doesn't she taste divine?" Ranto chuckled from his perch on the other side of the freaking room.

I wanted him closer. "Ranto."

"I know, mate. Why don't you lie back and let Hendrix feast first? Then we can all have some fun together." How could he be so calm when I was jittering out of my skin?

Hendrix seemed to be on the same wavelength as Ranto, and with a small tug, he guided me back to the mattress, hooked my leg over his shoulders, and began eating me like a man starved. I gasped and shuddered at the scrape of his beard over my sensitive flesh as he stroked me hard, not playing games in the pursuit of pleasure.

Locking eyes with Ranto, I saw the same hunger reflected back at me. He wasn't unaffected at all. He was showing me that he could share.

I couldn't have appreciated it more, especially as Hendrix thrust two fingers inside of me and pleasure washed through me. He sat up and wiped a hand down his beard, flicking his gaze to Ranto in invitation. Finally, my raiju was ready to play.

"Shuffle up on the bed, Treasure. Let him use your mouth."

I did as I was told, hanging my head off the edge of the bed and sticking my tongue out, so ready to taste him. Ranto smirked, leaned down, and sucked my tongue into his mouth, in a dirty upside-down kiss. When he pulled away, I wanted to follow him, but he clicked his tongue.

"Are you going to let Hendrix inside you?"

Hendrix cursed. "Condoms. I didn't think about it."

"It's fine," I said hurriedly. "I'm protected, so it's only if you want to use one."

If Hendrix's groan was anything to go by, I thought it was safe to say we were good. He stripped out of his clothes in record time, and I barely had time to appreciate his body before he blanketed mine.

"Are you sure?" he asked, eyeing me carefully as he positioned himself at my core.

"Absolutely." I hooked my heels behind his thighs and encouraged him to surge into me. Dropping my head back, I caught sight of Ranto, sweats pushed down around his thighs and erection in hand, pumping it slowly. My mouth dropped open on a moan as Hendrix pulled back on a long stroke and thrust back in hard.

Ranto slid a hand behind my head, lifting me to the angle he wanted before tapping my cheek with his hard cock. "Are you ready for me?"

I opened wide, smiling around his length as it slid easily into my throat. Upside-down blow jobs were so much easier on the throat.

It was the last coherent thought I had before the men found a rhythm between them that took my brain offline. I was so full. So connected with the men that all I could do was take all they gave to me and hope it kept coming. Hendrix adjusted his grip and began to pound into me as Ranto pulled out of my mouth so I could breathe.

"Are you going to come in her throat? Or do you want this hole when I'm done?"

I groaned at the lust that dripped from Hendrix's words, not at all concerned that he talked as though I wasn't there. If I said stop, they would. Immediately.

"Make sure you give it all to her. I want her dripping before I fuck it back inside." Ranto moved around the bed as Hendrix stiffened above me, burying his head in the crook of my neck as he growled through his orgasm.

When he pulled out, Ranto moaned, running his fingers through the mess left behind before he took over the position between my legs. My body was Jell-O. Floppy and sated. But when Ranto turned an assessing eye on me, I still held my arms out, ready to welcome him in me.

Using two fingers, he pumped into me slowly, his whole body shuddering at the squelching noise that came from my used pussy. Heat burned my cheeks, but I shook the emotion away. Why should I be embarrassed when he was so obviously turned on? Still, I couldn't keep myself from checking.

"You like it?"

He paused. Sharp eyes flicking to meet mine. "Babe, you have no idea how sexy you feel. How impatient I am to slide into this soft, wet heat that Hendrix has prepared for me. I'm taking a moment, so I don't come the second I get inside you."

"I mean... it's okay if you do."

His growl was more wolf than human as he finally let himself go, gripping my hips and slamming home before I could finish speaking. Gone was the careful lover. There was no finesse as he pounded into me, the obscene sounds coming from the collision of our bodies filling the room with a lust-drunk soundtrack. A hand brushed over my hair, and I rolled my head to the side to find Hendrix stretched out beside me, watching.

Ranto adjusted his angle and reached between us, pulling a whimper from me as he thumbed my oversensitive clit.

"Come on, babe. One more for me. I know you can do it. You're such a good girl for us."

That did it. My eyesight went white as my climax crashed over me. Ranto snarled as he followed me into bliss, and from far away, I heard a shout. I couldn't care too much about it as I drifted in a state of post-orgasmic bliss.

"Treasure."

My ears came back online a few moments later. When had I closed my eyes? I blinked them open lazily, slowly swimming up through the layers of dopamine flooding my system.

"Something's happening to Ranto."

That got me moving.

Sitting up quickly, I barely missed headbutting Hendrix, who pulled back just in time.

At the foot of the bed, Ranto stood, arms wide as sparks danced along his skin.

"I didn't do it," I blurted, wondering how he could look so full of power. Had I accidentally discharged during orgasm? I snorted. Technically, yes, I definitely had, but not electricity.

"What...?"

"I think my powers just came in." Ranto's voice was full of wonder, and it occurred to me I knew nothing about raiju.

"Another gap in your knowledge?" Hendrix asked.

I glared at him, silently asking for an explanation without the judgment, thank you.

"Raiju come into their powers when they find their mate. Usually after sexual intercourse." Beneath his curls, his ears colored. He could have a filthy three-way with us, but the mention of sex made him blush? Be still my heart, that was adorable. Because I had to do something to save the poor guy —or possibly make him blush harder—I decided to go to my tried-and-true coping mechanism. Humor.

"So what I'm hearing is I have a magical pussy. We should all get matching t-shirts. I'm sure Lindsay would be happy to bedazzle them for us."

A sharp jolt hit me in the butt, and I turned a scowl on the super-powered raiju in the room as I rubbed my poor, abused posterior.

"No. That's my trick. No zapping the zapper."

Ranto chuckled. "Turnabout is fair play, my love. Deal with it."

Shrugging back into the stupid Pikachu hoodie, he pulled

up his pants and left with a wink while I turned a dumbfounded look on Hendrix.

The ass was no help. He shrugged and began collecting his clothing before he, too, left with a quick kiss goodbye.

I lay back on the bed, completely naked and sated as my brain started to run hard, obsessing over the one little word I never expected to hear.

Love.

Ranto

"So, explain the plant thing to me again?" The buzzing in my veins felt almost as perfect as slipping the little ILY to Harlow after a mind-blowing orgasm. Ok, fine. So I hadn't said *I love you* specifically, but the sentiment was the same.

"I've literally been talking about it since the moment we met," Kylen groused.

Instead of pointing out the fact I'd spent ninety percent of the last week napping while he blathered, I focused on pushing small pulses of electricity through my fingertips.

"Look! Sparkler fireworks!" I grinned at the small crackles of electricity that bounced through the air at eye level.

"Ugh. Show off." Addie scowled from her slumped position against one of my many napping trees. When I sent her a questioning look, she rolled her eyes. "You've had powers—out of nowhere, BTW—for, like, five seconds, and you can do neat tricks with it. It's sus, dude."

"Sus?" I asked Kylen, who just shrugged.

"I don't speak teenage girl. Do you actually want to know about the plant?"

Not really, but I was good at solving mysteries. Maybe if he found his miracle cure, we could get on a roll and solve this curse thing, too. My gut told me he was right about us being here for a reason, because fate existed—fuck you very much, Hendrix—but I couldn't figure out the how of it all.

"Sure. Tell me while I try to make sheet lightning between my hands."

I brought my palms together and visualized the electric barriers that every sci-fi movie made in the last ten years used to demonstrate containment and imagined weaving a web stretching between each hand.

"It's a member of the nightshade family that is reported to grow in areas that have been exposed to high levels of magical disaster. What we know of the area makes it a good candidate for the conditions necessary for the growth."

I cursed as the energy snapped back and scorched my pinkie finger.

"But what does it look like? Smell like? Do you know what you're looking for exactly? Or just hoping you'll accidentally knock yourself out, wake up and be all *Eureka*!"

"Sure. This guy gets powers, and I'm stuck in dud witch land," Addie muttered.

"Jealous?" I asked, sending the tiniest spark to zap her grumpy butt.

She squeaked, harrumphed, and continued to gripe about her poor luck while I tuned her out to focus on Kylen.

"It only blooms under the light of the moon, or when threatened, to spread its pollen, which is the source of the sedative effect we're hoping to harness from the plant. Plant identification is difficult because many who have tried to find it have succumbed to the effects long before they could reach the bloom, but they did report a strong scent of candy floss and blue cheese on the breeze before losing consciousness. During the day, it looks like any other plant bulb except that its roots are blue."

"Candy floss and blue cheese sounds disgusting." Addie stood and stretched, ambling over to where Kylen kneeled. She dropped down beside him, and I zoned out, staring at their matching dirty blonde hair with unfocused eyes as I worked through the scent profile Kylen had described. I had smelled that before.

"Let's go for a walk," I said, offering a hand to pull Addie to her feet before doing the same for Kylen.

"Okay...?"

It was a decent walk into the woods, and I had a moment's hesitation.

"Actually, Addie. It's a bit far. Can you go hang with Harlow for a while?" My mate would kill me if anything happened to her chosen sister. I grabbed the girl's shoulders and gently pushed her in the direction of the town.

"But what if she's boning one of the others?"

Jealousy flared in my gut before I pushed it down again. My mate was a powerful witch who needed several mates. Just because I didn't like to share didn't mean I wouldn't. Plus, sharing her with Hendrix had been crazy hot. Maybe if I could solve all the mysteries, we could do it again.

"Then find Lindsay."

She made a rude noise but stomped uphill toward the town, her back ramrod straight and attitude pouring off her in waves so potent it was almost a form of power all on its own. Teenagers were scary.

Meeting Kylen's curious eyes, I nodded in the direction we needed to head and led the way.

We walked in silence for the first half hour, Kylen stopping periodically to inspect different leaves and shrubs. When he leaned close to one covered in small white flowers, I cringed, hoping it wasn't one of the ones I'd pissed on in my other form.

"So... Addie," I said, hoping to start up a conversation that didn't include my urine.

"She's a spitfire, isn't she?"

I hummed. That wasn't quite what I was talking about, but I wasn't sure how, or if, I should follow through on the thought forming in my mind.

Apparently, my brain-to-mouth filter had taken a vacation because, with very little finesse, the next words toppled out of my mouth. "She's your family. Biologically."

"What the actual fuck, dude? What are you talking about?"

How did he not understand it? He was the nature guy, for fuck's sake, and I'd made it as clear as I could.

"She's biologically related to you," I said, hoping that by saying it at half the speed, he'd have twice the understanding.

Kylen scowled at me. "You already said that. How could you possibly know that?"

He grabbed my arm, pulling me to a stop on the path. Did he want to find this plant, or not? I could be playing with electricity right now if it weren't for him. When he folded his arms, feet firmly planted and a single eyebrow almost in his hairline, I decided to spell it out for him so we could get moving again.

"You share a ridiculous number of genetic markers in your facial features and bone structure. Including the attached earlobes, single nostril flare when you're both angry, and dimples. You smell the same. You have the same hair and eye color. Not similar. The. Same. Also, and most definitive, I can taste the same genetic markers in your blood."

"When did you taste our blood?!"

"Keep your voice down. This isn't a question of who stole samples of whose blood while they slept to prove a point. This is about family. Long-lost family. It's like a lifetime movie!" I held my arms above my head, grinning widely in hopes he'd pick up on how exciting this moment should be for him.

Instead of cheering at my genius, he pinched the bridge of his nose like he had a headache.

"You know what? This isn't the time to deal with this." He pinned me with a hard look and pointed his finger in my face. "Do not bring this up with Addie yet. We'll deal with it after we've figured out how to break Harlow's curse. Okay?"

I shrugged. It was no skin off my nose what he did with the information. My motivation behind puzzling out the connection was a hunch that itched under my skin until I needed to prove myself right.

I loved solving mysteries, which was why I had the best job ever.

Considering Kylen got really quiet after my big reveal, I was glad the place we needed to go wasn't that far away. The trees began to feel familiar as I pictured following Harlow through the woods, her panic an acidic tang in the air. I'd been distracted by a scent on... I looked ahead and found the rock that had taken my attention the first time here and beside it...

"Oh, hell yeah. I thought I lost this." My puppy pack was under a creeping vine beside the rock. Inside was a change of clothes, a couple of snacks, and my cell phone. "Damn. It's dead. Think anyone has a charger back at the motel?"

Kylen watched me, eyes wide in bewilderment. Shit, that was right. Stinky plant. I closed my eyes, picturing the scene. Harlow over there, punk ass wolf on top of her, absorbing her magic. The wind shifted from the northwest to the south, and the smell came from...

"There!" I pointed to a grayish green pod that stuck out of a sheet of moss wedged under a boulder.

Kylen took a step forward, then another, before falling to

his knees and digging in the dirt like a man possessed. He sifted through the earth until a spot of blue appeared.

"It's... Holy shit. You found it." Kylen's face was so pale, it made me glad he was already sitting so he wouldn't fall over.

"That's it, then?" I asked, opening an emergency Twinkie.

He surged to his feet, grasped me by the shoulders, and pressed his lips hard against mine. My first reaction was to protect my treat, but when it became obvious this was gratitude, not food theft, I waited him out. He pulled back and glanced over his shoulder at his prize.

"I know we're going to be sharing a mate and all that, but I don't swing that way. You might be better off talking to Bruin," I said through a mouthful of Twinkie.

He winked, color slowly returning to his face. "Don't worry. I've got that covered."

I barked a laugh as he turned his attention to claiming his prize before we walked back to town in companionable silence.

***

We returned to the motel in good spirits while the sun was still in the sky, for a change, so that Kylen could pot his new plant pet to study. Harlow sat with him, watching him with interest as he worked.

"I don't totally get it, but it's cute the way he gets so excited!"

Lindsay and Addie stretched out on the queen bed and turned on some reality television show, while Bruin sat in a corner, pretending to bitch about the choice while conveniently commentating on the characters by name. Hendrix had gone to stretch his wings while I curled up beside the bed and let Addie stroke my head absently. Human or dog, I defy anyone to say they don't like having their head stroked.

A noise outside heralded Hendrix's return, but the quick open and close of the next room's door set me on alert. I slid out from beneath Addie's hand, then slipped through to the adjoining room with Harlow.

"We have a problem," Hendrix said, pulling the curtains closed. "There is a whole pack of bikers headed this way. I couldn't make out the club on their cuts, but there's only one group I know you have beef with."

The three of us glanced at the wall to next door, while Kylen paused in his work, spinning in the chair to face us.

"We need to bring everyone in on this," Hendrix said. "Especially if Bruin's the one who called them in."

Harlow shook her head. "He wouldn't, and it'd be better to keep him out of the way. Let the club think he isn't involved. What I need is for you to keep Addie safe while I deal with this. Promise me."

Movement in the doorway caught my attention, but when I glanced over, there was nothing but the blonde tips of someone's hair disappearing back into the other room.

I stayed quiet with Kylen while Hendrix and Harlow went back and forth for a few minutes on the best course of action. Basically, Hendrix was being reasonable, and my mate acted like she had a death wish. Not that I was biased at all. We had no way of knowing the power these bikers were packing, but Harlow was adamant.

"I've dealt with them before, and I can do it again." She spoke through gritted teeth, trying to keep her voice low so as not to alert the other room of the situation. "Seriously, Hendrix, you better back off, or I swear I'll fry your balls so bad they'll twitch any time you so much as think the word electricity."

Despite my newfound electrical abilities, even I wouldn't have tried her on that one. As she disappeared through the door, the three of us shared a helpless look. No one in the other room would be happy with us letting her walk out.

Her wishes were clear. Keep Addie safe. But that didn't mean we couldn't still help.

"Does anyone have a charger? My phone is dead," I said.

Hendrix looked at me like I was crazy. "Is now really the time?"

"Absolutely." I grinned. "I need to make a call."

July 16th, 1674

My children are dead.

One by one, I discovered their lifeless bodies, each of them drained of magic, and had my heart ripped out.

My lovers are torn. Some prepare for war, yearning to avenge our children, while others want to wait and grieve our losses. I am tired of grieving. My tears have dried, and all I have left is the pit of anguish at my core.

I do not wish to take my lover's choices from them, but this battle is mine. I allowed this darkness to encroach upon our land for years, and as a result, my darling children paid the price. If I do not act now, the coven's future will truly be lost.

Memories I thought long forgotten plague my mind. Instances where I could have prevented these tragedies, had I only been more forceful. Been more willing to do what was needed. Yet instead, I remained under the misguided illusion that peaceful resolutions were possible. How disgustingly foolish of me.

My children's killer sought my fury, and by the goddess, he shall have it.

Morfran. The so-called sorcerer of Spells Hollow.

Every time I close my eyes, I see his wicked grin. The devious smile he wore as each of my children's bodies were carried away. Cries filled the air, but not from him. He simply stared into my broken heart and promised me it was only the beginning.

Our seer has predicted a blood moon tomorrow night, and Morfran has requested a meeting in the town square. I'm sure it is no coincidence. This is where he'll enact his plot, whatever that may be. He wants me standing at my most powerful before he attempts to bring me to my knees. But as I'm sure he knows, with my children gone and my lovers fighting amongst each other over our next steps, I am also at my most vulnerable.

This morning, I ordered the townspeople to flee. A few families, notably those with children, have taken their belongings, and now head for New Amsterdam. However, many are reluctant to abandon their homes. Though I wish they would reconsider, I do not blame them. Our families built these homes as a sanctuary from our oppressors. It feels so wrong for them to start over again, but hopefully they won't have to.

When the moon rises tonight, I shall traverse the catacombs beneath the town and reinforce the wards wherever I can. In the event of my death, they should ensure the safety of my witches. Or at least, delay the destruction long enough for them to escape.

My hand shakes as I write this. I fear not only for the coven, but for the generations to come. By murdering children, Morfran has made it clear that my generation of witches shall not be the only ones made to suffer. However, I swear I shall give my life before another soul is harmed by his darkness.

The Nightshade line may now end with me, but one way or another, I will ensure my coven lives on.

Harlow

No one was going to take my new family from me, and I was going to cut a biker bitch who tried.

Gravel crunched beneath my boots as I stomped across the parking lot and headed toward the highway. I didn't want to chance Addie seeing what was about to go down, because if the power running through my limbs was anything to go by, I was about to stop the hearts of every single one of those men. All I wanted was to be a good role model for her, and even I knew that committing mass murder wasn't something you should teach a kid.

Maybe when she was older.

Lightning arced from my fingertips, and I sent up a silent prayer of thanks that the dirt road didn't conduct electricity. A blackout at the hotel would have given me away for sure.

As I reached the highway, I closed my eyes, listening for the rumble on the breeze that would announce the arrival of the cavalry.

A small, insecure part of me whispered that maybe Bruin really had betrayed me. That maybe, even now, he waited for the signal to come and finish his mission in front of a live audience. I wasn't sure I had it in me to hurt him the way I intended to hurt his club, and that thought alone was enough to make me realize how much the asshole had grown on me.

A fine vibration trembled up through my feet before that deep growl I'd been waiting for broke the peaceful silence and royally fucked up my day.

Planting my feet in the middle of the road, I folded my arms and pasted a nasty smirk on my face. Show no fear. After that, there was nothing left to do but wait.

On the horizon, small black dots resolved themselves into two long lines of motorcycles. Naww… I guessed Kevy-bear was scared of being beaten by a girl again and had brought all his friends to try to prevent it. Too bad for him, I didn't know the meaning of surrender.

The MC closed in fast and skidded to a stop in front of me with a shower of gravel that scuffed my boots and bounced painfully off my cheeks.

"Well, well, well. Fancy seeing an ass like you in a place like this," I drawled, running my eyes slowly over his posse before focusing on Mr Big, Dumb, and Insecure himself.

"We came to watch you die, bitch. I hope you've made your funeral arrangements." He hefted his sweaty bulk off his poor bike, mutton chops quivering with barely suppressed hatred.

I flexed my hands, willing my power to stay hidden.

"This is a long way to come for the sake of your fragile ego. Are you compensating for something over there, Kevy-bear?" I crooked my pinkie finger at him, pouting in mock sympathy.

"Fuck you, bi—"

A weaselly guy caught his arm, shaking his head emphatically as the MC president lunged for me.

"Easy, big guy." I laughed, holding up both hands. Should I have been antagonizing the boss of all these surly looking bikers? No. But damn if it wasn't fun.

As we bantered—hey, death threats could be banter; it just

wasn't as sexy as when Bruin did it—I was aware of his companions dismounting and slowly circling me until any escape route was cut off. I wasn't worried, knowing I could make my own path. Bruin hadn't expected my powers the first time we'd fought, so unless he'd fed them intel in the last couple of weeks, they shouldn't know how powerful I really am.

"Game on, bitches. Who wants to go first?" I cocked my fists, prepared to keep up the pretense for as long as I could.

The way my skin buzzed told me it wouldn't be long, but hopefully, I could have some fun first. The thump of boots on the road's hard surface signaled the start of the brawl as a tall biker tried to attack me from behind. I stepped aside as he approached, aiming a kick at his crotch before I bounced out of the way of his friend coming in from the other side. Landing a heavy hit to a third guy's cheek, I chanced a glance around to look for a gap in the attacks to slip through and caught a knee to the ribs.

When the heroes in movies were attacked by droves of villains, the bad guys each waited their turn for an ass kicking, hovering in a circle and closing in in groups of two or three so the hero could dispatch them appropriately. This... was bedlam. Limbs flew everywhere, some making contact with me, others nowhere near, which made me wonder if they were passing time fighting each other if they couldn't reach me. I didn't have time to find out one way or the other as my power built inside me, ready to defend against the waves of attack.

With a war cry, I let loose a shock wave of energy and took my first deep breath since the brawl began, but the men kept coming, and the next wave pounded into them without my conscious say-so.

That's concerning.

The road beneath our feet rumbled, and clods of dirt rose into the air. Breaking free of the guy swinging a crowbar at my knees, I looked around and cursed.

The weasel guy was an earth witch.

With a flick of his wrist, the chunks of earth became missiles locked on target. I dropped to my belly and sent a jagged bolt of electricity toward all those lovely, conductible metal vehicles. Kevy-Bear yelped, knocking into weasel boy, and—thankfully—destroying his concentration.

I need more energy.

The lightning came faster this time. The volume, like nothing I'd experienced before, poured out until it swirled around me in a vortex of electrical energy. My hair stood on end, the energy zapping off goosebumps that ran up and down my arms.

A vague warning echoed in the back of my mind. A feeling that the power was too much. Too unstable. My heart pounded as the energy creeped through my feet and coated the road before me.

What had felt freeing a moment before took a painful turn as my muscles cramped under the strain.

Too much. Too much. Too much.

It became a fearful chant as bikers ran before the bolts of lightning that licked out of my body without my intention. Bodies littered the road around me in a circle, the smell of scorched flesh and leather heavy in the air.

With a lurch, my heart seized, and I screamed in agony as my power exploded out of me in a wave of devastation. Choking on a sob, I tried again to pull the energy back into me, like I had with Ranto and Kylen's help. I prayed for the peace that usually came with discharging my power, but it only pulled harder at my core, tearing me apart from the inside.

This was what Levina had experienced in that death loop.

This is how my mother had died the night of the riot.

It was how I would die, too.

A single tear tracked down my burning face as I accepted the reality of my fate.

The curse had claimed another witch.

Kylen

"Is Addie in here with you?" Lindsay's voice jolted me out of my thoughts as I sat in front of the plant I'd been searching for my entire life while thinking about the life of a certain lightning witch that was under threat.

We shouldn't have let her go off alone. My gut churned at the idea of her taking on an entire MC by herself, even with her powers. I was a lover, not a fighter, so I'd have been no help, but maybe Bruin could, if he didn't turn around and follow through with his threats to kill her.

I sighed, dropping my head in my hands as Ranto said goodbye to his friend.

"They're two hours away, but with lights and sirens, they might get here faster."

Two hours was too long to wait. Anxiety itched at the back of my mind as I turned back to my plant. Could I harvest the pollen and use it against the entire club? How would we get Harlow out before we did it? I had full faith in Harlow's ability to look after herself, but she shouldn't have had to. It was why we were here. I was sure of it.

A deep cough pulled my wayward mind back to the doorway.

"Addie?" Lindsay asked, propping a hand on his hip.

"We thought she was with you," Ranto said, frowning over at me as my gut dropped through the floor.

"No, she went for candy a little while ago and didn't come back. She's probably found some kind of trouble to get into."

A chiming filled the wary silence in the room following that statement, and Lindsay retrieved his cell, answering as though he hadn't felt the energy shift.

"Hey, sexy. Did you predict I'd be thirsty for a little phone session today?" The teasing look dropped from his eyes in an instant as a deep voice murmured through the phone. Whatever the caller was saying, it was serious.

Beneath our feet, the earth rumbled in a way it shouldn't have so far from a fault line.

That couldn't be good.

"Fuck it. She can fry my balls all she wants, as long as she's alive to do it," Hendrix muttered as he dove for the door.

Ranto followed, with Lindsay close behind, talking a mile a minute to whoever the caller was. I paused, then backtracked to the other room.

"Harlow's facing your crew, and we think she's in trouble. Are there going to be questions about your allegiance? Or should I tie you up right now?"

Bruin leaped to his feet, closing the distance between us until the length of his body pressed against mine.

"The only time you ever need to tie me up is when you're planning on pounding my prostate again, lover."

I let my mouth stretch into a sharp grin and reached around to take his ass in a possessive hold.

"Good boy."

His whole body shuddered, and I wished I had time to enjoy the reaction, but we had work to do. Hitting the parking lot at a sprint, we put on a burst of speed to catch up to Lindsay and Hendrix.

"Kedron said we need to hurry," Lindsay panted.

"Who the fuck is Kedron?" Bruin growled, passing Lindsay easily.

"He's my boss-turned-fuck-buddy-maybe-love who refuses to label what we have even though he'll never do better than—"

"Lindsay, focus. Why are we listening to some dude who isn't here?"

"Oh! He's psychic. Basically, he said it's time for you bitches to step up and help break the curse."

I stumbled over my own feet, gaping at Lindsay for a moment before kicking back into a sprint.

The intersection to the highway was two hundred feet away. One hundred feet. Fifty.

A scream tore through the air. I skidded to a halt beside Hendrix and watched in horror as a pulse of energy ripped from Harlow's skin in a crackling circle of blue. Leather clad bikers fell all around her as she sobbed, her body appearing to pulse with electricity.

"Addie." Lindsay's voice cracked as he stumbled up behind us and crashed to his knees.

"What—?" I followed his line of sight and felt my heart stop as I noticed the small blonde body lying far too still at the edge of Harlow's raging lightning.

"Shit." I lunged for her body, lashing out when I was pulled up short by a firm hand.

"We have to get to Harlow," Bruin growled, eyes set on the center of the electrical storm.

"She's my sister!" I screamed, throwing my weight around in an attempt to break his grip.

"They'll both die if we don't help her stop." Bruin shook me, turning us both toward where Harlow had collapsed to her knees.

A body knocked me from the side, and Ranto strode past me, straight into the eye of the storm. Bruin's grip tightened for a moment before he stepped away and followed Ranto's lead.

"As soon as you can, get Addie clear. We'll do what we have to to get Harlow out of this," I yelled to Lindsay, then locked eyes with Hendrix. His lips ticked up in an almost smile, which I returned immediately. We were doing this.

Passing through the electrical field was like being hit with a taser, and I gritted my teeth, willing my muscles not to seize as the simple act of walking became a challenge. The hair on the back of my neck stood on end, and painful jolts licked at my skin. Beside me, Hendrix wasn't faring much better. His lip was curled in a pain-filled snarl as his hands curled into claws. After a few seconds, which seemed to stretch for decades, there was a hiccup in the howling energy. I lurched forward to find Ranto wrapped around Harlow's body. His white hair sparked with energy while his eyes, pinched at the corners with pain, glowed neon blue.

"He's absorbing the energy," I muttered.

Bruin stepped up next and placed his hands on her temples. Her face rippled, a serene mask slipping over her features as her body lost some of its rigidity.

"Are you going to help us? Or just watch?" Ranto growled, his voice nothing more than a strained rasp.

I shook my head and stepped in to place a hand over Harlow's stomach. The solar plexus was the center of emotion and was posited to be the source of a witch's magic. With a deep breath for focus, I pulled at the jagged pieces of power I could feel in her and channeled it in through my body and out through my feet into the ground.

"Thank God," Ranto breathed beside me, and I noticed the cyclone of energy had begun to dissipate.

"Harlow?" Bruin's voice held a note of panic.

Her face was ashen, the lightning pulsing out of her in fits and spurts that Ranto and I fought to contain, but there was something wrong. We were losing her.

"Shit. Harlow!" I pressed my hand hard into her stomach, feeding my magic back into her in hopes it could revive her, but she only slumped further into Ranto's hold.

"You were right. She does need us all. This is..." Hendrix trailed off, still not quite able to say the word fate.

I didn't particularly care about his beliefs, only that as he placed a hand over her heart, a golden glow lit up at their point of connection.

"Come back to us, Treasure. We need you."

A hard tug on my magic startled me. The trickle I'd been feeding into her became a stream, and as I looked at the men around me, I got the distinct impression we were all having the same experience.

An eerie silence hung in the air, sparking like dust motes as time ground to a halt. Beyond the circle of devastation, Lindsay kneeled with Addie unconscious in his lap, their bodies a tableau vivant of grief. Behind them stood two figures, almost transparent and unnervingly familiar. Their likeness hung in the study of Harlow's ancestor's house, a reminder of the original owners. I turned my attention back to Harlow, terrified the shades had come to witness the curse finish her off.

The golden light burned brighter under Hendrix's hand until I was forced to shield my eyes.

And then it was gone.

A cool breeze swept over my heated skin, carrying the lingering scent of ozone.

My skin buzzed as the last of the power funneled into the earth, and my sight blurred with tears at the sight of still, blue lips... that opened on a heavy gasp.

Harlow

My mind swam in an ocean of peace. Drifting on lazy currents, thoughts surfaced and slipped away like debris swirling at the water's whim. Ripples formed around me as I moved through warm eddies that kept me far from the bank and what I might find above the surface. Pressure at my temples, heart, and stomach comforted me, reminding me of something I couldn't quite grasp.

It's time to finish this, little lightning rod. You must go back and see it done.

The voice pierced through me like a jolt of electricity, shocking me out of my daze. My head broke the surface of the water, and as I took a gulp of air, I felt a tear at the center of my being.

Be strong, little one. It's time to let go.

I looked up into my own face and blinked in confusion. How could I encourage myself? Levina. The name stuck in my mind a moment before Donahue stepped up beside her.

We're here with you always. Now stop fighting and let them in.

Stop fighting who? The pressure over my heart increased, and an image of a huge lion with an eagle's head roared through my mind's eye. Vines crept around my waist, contracting my stomach as water continued to flow over my head. At my back, I felt loyalty and connection, and with the acknowledgement of them, my men appeared. Surrender was both the easiest and hardest thing I'd ever done as I embraced the sensations each brought out in me and felt my world click into place.

The next gasp of air came far more painfully than the first, but that seemed to be a good indication I'd made my way back to consciousness. A drop of moisture hit my hand, and I looked up into the earnest blue eyes of my nature witch.

"Welcome back," he whispered, casting a glance over his shoulders. He turned back with a small frown creasing his brow.

My heart ached, but my body hummed with an energy unlike anything I'd ever felt. It was powerful in a way that could put my previously wild magic to shame, but with smoother, more manageable edges.

"Holy shit. The curse is broken."

Hendrix nodded at my wide-eyed stare. "Yeah, we think so. How do you feel?"

I turned my attention inward, and smiled as I felt the presence of each one of my men, where previously there had only been chaotic energy. There was no way to properly quantify the feelings bubbling up inside of me, so I settled for the most apt.

"Alive."

Hendrix returned my grin before moving away to make room for Bruin.

"How about you don't pull the lone cowboy shit again and scare us half to death, huh?"

"That almost sounded like a compliment."

"Perish the thought." His eyes crinkled in the corners before he, too, straightened and moved away.

"Please don't scare us like that again." Ranto's voice rumbled through my back, making me acutely aware of the fact I seemed to be using him as a human pillow. Before I could decide on whether to go for a sweet or smartass reply, the sound of my name pulled at our attention.

Ten feet from where I lay, Lindsay sat with his back to me, his wide shoulders curled over.

"What...?" I sat up, and the change of angle showed me a slightly melted pair of Converse shoes.

"Addie!" Scrambling over on hands and knees, I almost shoved my best friend out of the way with my urgency to reach her.

"What happened? What do I do? Shit. This is my fault. Addie, can you hear me?"

A warm hand pressed against my back, and then Kylen crouched beside me.

"Lindsay got her heart beating again with CPR, but it's not beating the way it should. She's in and out of consciousness. You're going to have to shock her again."

My chest heaved as I struggled to get air into my lungs. Shocking her had put her in this position. How the hell was doing the same thing going to get her out of it?

"I can't do it. My power is too violent. Too much. I can't do it."

"Hey." Kylen's voice was harder than I'd ever heard it as he squeezed my shoulder. "I'm not going to see my sister die because you had a panic attack when you could have helped her. Take a breath and think. It's the same as using a defibrillator, just that you're a person instead. Put your hands on her. One over her chest, the other wrapping around her ribs. Good. Just like that. Now, you're going to send a single pulse through her." He looked around, waving Lindsay back so everyone was clear. "Now."

With a prayer to whoever the fuck was up there listening, I sent a jolt of power out through my palms. Addie's small body seized in a convulsion that made my stomach turn. When she flopped to the ground, Kylen checked her pulse.

"One more."

We repeated the action and this time, Addie's lashes fluttered.

"Ow. Who the hell hit me? I think I bruised a rib. Harlow! You're ok. I was going to save you."

I choked on a sob as I crushed her to me in a hard hug, feeling the strong, steady beat of her heart beneath my hands. She was okay. She was safe. She was...

"What the hell?" I asked, eyeing the small carpet of white flowers that spread beneath her palm.

"Did you do that?"

Addie glanced down at her hand, a look of awe dawning on her face as she touched a finger to one of the buds and drew a coiling vine from its center.

"I have powers?" she breathed so quietly I wondered if she worried it would disappear if she were too loud.

"My sister has the same powers as me!" Kylen crowed, scooping Lindsay into a hug.

"Sister?!" Addie shrieked, flowers forgotten for the moment. My nature witch took a half step toward her, rubbing the back of his neck in an endearingly nervous way.

"Ahh... yeah. So, you see. Ranto—Oof!" Kylen cut off mid explanation as he struggled to catch ninety-two pounds of flying teenager.

"I have a family!" Addie grinned over her shoulder at me from the koala grip she had on her brother.

I smiled indulgently at her but couldn't help pointing out, "You've always had a family. Now you just have a few more."

Her breathing hitched, and I pretended not to notice as she surreptitiously wiped her face on Kylen's shirt.

"*We'll talk about this later,*" I mouthed at him.

He shot me a sheepish smile as she hopped out of his arms and walked toward my biker, who stood at the edge of the action, seemingly unsure what to do.

"Hey, Bruin, guess what! Now I can tie you up in vines, too." Addie called, earning a wince from him and a hearty chorus of *No* from the rest of us.

"We still have an hour to wait, and some of these bastards are starting to stir." Ranto wasn't paying attention to the proceedings as he directed Hendrix to check on each of the unconscious bikers. He swiped a hand down his face, looking tired, yet determined, but something in his statement caught my attention.

"What are we waiting for?"

I hadn't known about Ranto's job as a PI, but the lack of surprise on Kylen's face told me it was old news to him. He explained how he'd been privately contracted to assist a task force in the takedown of the Grim Hearts MC chapter that happened to be littering the highway at present, and how he'd put out the call for reinforcements the second we caught wind of their attack.

Bruin snorted, eyeing Ranto closely, but only received an enigmatic grin in return. I understood his worry. The only reason Ranto could have been on the case he described and end up following me was because of him. I reached out and took his hand, waiting for him to make eye contact.

"Whatever happens, we'll deal with it together."

He grunted, but his fingers tightened in a return squeeze.

"Well, it won't be worth much if they all take off before the task force gets here," Ranto groused.

We needed time. And for the assholes to stay asleep.

Or sedated.

"Kylen!" I shouted, wincing as the sound echoed in the quiet air. "Your plant."

Understanding washed over his face, and with a quick look at Addie, they both took off toward the motel.

"I really hope that plant of his doesn't accidentally kill them all," Bruin muttered.

I glanced at him, trying to read his tone. He said he was sure of his allegiances, but there was a line in the sand that seemed to include a level of mortality on both sides.

"We don't want to get stuck with a murder charge because of experimental medicine," he clarified, taking in my worried expression.

I coughed a laugh and elbowed him. He responded by hooking an arm around my neck and planting a kiss on my head. Sweet bastard. Not that I'd ever tell him that.

"Get off me, asshole. We need to keep your butt buddies asleep until they get to jail." There was no heat behind my words, and he chucked me on the chin before wandering off to help with the damage assessment.

In a surprisingly short amount of time, Kylen and Addie returned, the latter bouncing around her new brother like an excitable puppy, her mouth running a mile a minute while he held a jar like it was explosive. Maybe it was. I glanced toward Lindsay, silently encouraging him to distract our excitable ward so Kylen could save our asses.

"I'm so excited to see how this goes," he muttered, crouching beside the nearest biker, who was twitching like he was coming around.

Kylen sprinkled a small amount of the powder into his nostrils, and the movement ceased immediately.

"Harlow, can you monitor his pulse? I'll get the ones who

are stirring now, but I want to make sure it's safe before I use it on the rest of them."

I opened my mouth to reply but was interrupted by the blessed sound of sirens. Pressing two fingers beneath the meaty biker's jaw, I found his pulse beat strong and steady, then nodded to Kylen as he worked his way around to a few of the more conscious-looking men.

A phalanx of cars screeched to a halt behind the lines of bikes, and uniformed men swarmed the road in full SWAT gear. As the droves of men stumbled to a stop at the sight of unconscious bikers everywhere, a man in a well-fitted gray suit let out a low whistle.

"Looks like you guys have already had all the fun."

Ranto's face lit up. "Mikey! You came in person." He closed the distance between them, pulling the man into an enthusiastic hug. "Hey! You have to meet my mate." And then they were headed my way.

I'd always had a love-hate relationship with officers of the law. Mostly hate, seeing as they were responsible for screwing over runaway orphans and took issue when we stole to survive. Killjoys. But this was Ranto's friend, and for him, I'd make an effort.

"So, I guess we owe you thanks. Toto here tells me you're responsible for bringing down the Grim Hearts."

"Holy shit! Yes. That's sticking," Addie squealed, laughter bubbling out of her as she leaned on a grinning Lindsay.

Heat rose in my cheeks. Could I really take credit for almost succumbing to a curse and letting them all get caught in the fallout? Eh, why not.

"You're welcome."

Mike chuckled, looking around at us all.

"As much as we appreciate what you've done, we need to

ask you to leave us to the arrests. This is now an active crime scene." He glanced at Bruin with a frown.

"Why is he conscious? Bruin. Get down on the ground with your hands behind your head. You have the right to remain silent—"

"What?" I demanded, shooting a concerned look at Ranto.

Bruin had helped. Bruin was... well... not good. But he was mine.

Bruin sank to his knees, offering his wrists for cuffs and patiently waiting out the reading of his rights while sending me comforting glances.

"Mike," Ranto said, gripping his friend's shoulder.

"He's the club's enforcer and a legacy. He *is* the Grim Hearts MC. Give me one good reason why he shouldn't rot in jail with the rest of them."

Ranto flicked a look between Bruin and me before focusing back on his friend.

"He was my primary informer."

Bruin choked on a denial he couldn't quite squash, but Ranto talked over him. "He was instrumental in the demise of the club, and most importantly, he's bound to my mate. I have complete confidence in vouching for the strength of his allegiances. If he steps out of line, I'll rip him apart myself."

Mike stared at him for so long I began fantasizing about jailbreaks to retrieve my man from custody, but eventually the click of cuffs being released caught my ears.

"All of you, get out of here and let us do our jobs. If there's any trouble now or in the future from the enforcer, it's on your head."

Ranto nodded at his friend, then pulled him in for one more hug before we all turned back toward the motel. Kylen held back a little longer to explain the sedative to the officers and exchanged phone numbers so they could report on the effects.

Hendrix offered to stop off at the diner and get food for everyone, while Lindsay, Bruin, and Addie settled in to watch a trashy reality television show. Ranto shifted into his raiju form and curled his bulk around Addie, as though he still needed the reassurance that she was okay.

I waited by the door for Kylen to return, and as soon as he was in reaching distance, I cupped his face and pulled him into a devastating kiss. Pushing my tongue into his mouth, I tried to tell him without words how much he meant to me. How much I wanted him. The passion with which he returned the kiss stole the breath from my lungs and made all kinds of dirty fantasies kick off in my mind. I'd just decided that closing the adjoining room's door would give us adequate privacy when Hendrix cleared his throat loudly.

"Eat each other later. Right now, everyone needs real food."

I laughed, stepping away to let him through and flopped down at the small table, knocking Melisande's diary to the floor. As I retrieved the book, a loose page slipped from its place, tucked in the back cover.

The writing was done in a different hand, and curiosity burned through me. Was this the end of the story? Or a new mystery to solve? With the curse broken, tomorrow would be spent planning our next move. Would we head to our respective homes? Would they come with me? I hoped so, but how could I ask them to pick up their whole lives so that they could all share little old me?

I looked around, realizing Kylen had followed the food into the other room, and for the moment, I was alone.

Praying this wasn't the curiosity that killed the cat, I took a seat and started to read.

1655

The coven is gone.

In the days since the Sorcerer took our beloved priestess in a wicked blast of dark magic that razed all but the most protected corners of Spells Hollow, the families of our Priestess's consorts have had the most devastating and deadly of curses fall upon them.

I came upon Levina Torann crying over the corpse of her brother, Donahue, consort to the high priestess. His once handsome features were warped and burned. I am ashamed to admit I hurried on with my chores while the sounds of the lady's grief echoed through my bones.

The cows have lost their milk, and the chickens refuse to lay. The talk of the very land having absorbed the curse was incessant.

The first families left under the cover of darkness, the moon bearing witness as they slunk away from the home our mothers made a safe haven for all.

Safe haven no more.

Those who have not yet succumbed to the curse have fled in hopes of escaping its devastating reach.

We who are cursed... there is no escape. I know this in my core, but still I write this in hopes that future generations may bear witness to the words laid down by our priestess and know that we lived and loved.

The sorcerer took our future, and I believe sealed his own fate at the same time.

You who read this know that no curse can withstand the strength of love.

We will endure.

We shall return.

Harlow

The air buzzed with the promise of a storm coming tonight. Dark clouds covered the sky, blocking the sun's summer heat and making my fingers tingle. No sparks, though. I only did that on command now.

I waltzed through the doors to Cassandra's Bane as the cleaners worked to remove the evidence of last night's debauchery, then hopped up onto a bar stool next to the owner.

"I want my job back."

Kedron's mouth quirked up at one corner, but he didn't look up at me from his open folder of stock delivery forms. "And why's that?"

"What do you mean 'why'? I've worked here since I turned eighteen, and I'm good at it. You know I am."

"That's not a reason." He scribbled his signature at the bottom of a form and closed the folder, spinning on the stool to face me properly. "I employed you here because I saw potential in you and knew it would guide you in the right direction. But now your curse is broken. You have your whole life ahead of you, something no one in your family has had in centuries. Why do you want to spend it working security at a nightclub?"

"Steady income and an excuse to throw out drunken douchebags?"

He raised an eyebrow, unimpressed by the flippant answer.

Sliding off the stool, I moved to the other side of the bar and poured myself a soda while I thought about it. Why did I want my old job back? It had felt so obvious when I left the apartment earlier.

"It's what I've always done," I said slowly. "This job is my outlet."

Kedron nodded. "Your outlet for your unstable magic and the rage you never learned to deal with."

"Yikes! Don't hold back, boss. Tell me how you really feel."

"Neither of those things pose a problem for you now, so why do you still need an outlet?"

I sipped my soda and gave him a mock glare. A philosophical discussion over my life choices hadn't been on the agenda for today.

He smiled, joining me behind the bar and grabbing a pair of shot glasses. "You'll always have a place here, if you want it. I never filled your position, and honestly, you'd be doing me a favor to take it back. I've been borrowing staff from Eclipse ever since you left."

"Since you fired me," I corrected him.

"Potato, po-tah-to."

"No one says 'po-tah-to'." As I watched him pour two measures of tequila, I asked, "If the position is vacant, why does it sound like you don't want me to come back?"

He gave me an enigmatic smile that made my eye twitch. "I want to be sure that it's what you want, now that things have changed for you. Take your time to think. Talk it over with your boyfriends." He slid one of the glasses over to me. "Discover your future."

I bit my lip and thought about his words. He was right.

Things had changed for me. I'd changed. Not just the multiple lovers—though they were a fantastic bonus—but for the first time in my life, I felt like I had a chance at a real future for myself, and for my family.

"I want a part time management position."

"Oh? Got plans for the other half of your day?"

"College," I answered. "I could afford to start classes with the money from my promotion, and then I'll be ready for when you wanna hand me the keys to this place."

"Wow. Getting a bit ahead of yourself there, aren't you?"

I shook my head. "Nope. You've talked about wanting to open another club, maybe two, right? I'm gonna be ready."

Kedron grinned and held up his glass. I clinked it with mine and downed the shot, reveling in the burn down to my stomach.

"You can start training tomorrow night." He waved me away from the bar. "Now get out of my club while it's still mine. My newest bartender is outside, waiting to give you a ride home."

"Creepy. Thank you." I downed the last of my soda and headed for the door, before swiveling on my toe and calling back, "Oh, and talk to Lindsay. If you keep playing this boss-with-benefits schtick, you'll lose him."

He nodded, his expression sincere. "I won't let that happen."

As I made my way outside, I paused at the entrance, staring up at the gray sky. I used to hate how much it rained here. But as the scent of petrichor filled my senses, all I felt was contentment... and something digging into my lower back.

"Is that a knife poking my spine, or are you just happy to see me?"

Tattooed arms wrapped around me as my favorite biker

kissed my neck. "No knife this time, Sparky. But I've been told it's a weapon."

Laughter bubbled out of me. "Since when do you have jokes? Wait, you're Kedron's new bartender?"

He spun me in his arms, moving his hands down to cup my ass cheeks and press me against the hard lines of his body. "Well, I need the money after my last job didn't go so well. I fell for the target, and when the time came, I couldn't betray her."

Pushing up on my toes, I wrapped my arms around his neck and pulled him down for a bruising kiss. Oh, there was no way I was going to be able to keep my hands off him on shift. Holy shit, I was gonna be his boss. We'd be worse than Lindsay and Kedron within a week, and I couldn't wait.

"Come on," he mumbled against my lips. "I've got a present for you."

He took my hand and led me across the street to his bike, where he'd balanced a black helmet with painted lightning bolts on the seat. "I figured since we might be commuting together now, you should look the part."

I grabbed it, practically bouncing on my toes with glee. "You're so cute when you're not trying to kill me!"

He rolled his eyes and helped me put it on, tightening the strap under my chin until he was satisfied. "Don't worry. I'll keep hating you in the bedroom."

My heart fluttered. "Promise?"

"I'll fucking despise you, if it makes you happy."

***

When we arrived at my apartment building, we found Kylen and Addie sitting on the small patch of grass outside. The lack of sunlight didn't even bother them; they were so engrossed in their chat. It was sweet to see them connecting as siblings. As much as I loved that I had Lindsay while growing up, having a blood relative would have been incredible, and I was so happy Addie had found one. The fact that it was Kylen only made it better. I knew he'd be the best sibling to her, even though he'd be competing with me and Lindsay. I'd still be number one.

Kylen waved us over to sit with them, as he continued talking. "Yeah, I remember Mom being pregnant, but I was told the baby died in the accident. When my parents—sorry, *our* parents—died, I was left by myself and went to live with my aunt on our dad's side."

He smiled to himself, watching her run her hands over the grass and leave a trail of fresh daisies in her path. She'd taken to her new magic like she'd been using it for years.

"I don't remember much of what happened. I was fourteen at the time and not exactly coping. But the lawyer we've hired thinks they separated us when I went into foster care for a few days, before going to my aunt's. I didn't even know you were born."

Tears welled in his eyes, and he blinked them away. "Anyway, once I have a permanent address, your case worker thinks I have a real shot at being assigned your legal guardian."

Addie's jaw dropped, "You...want me to live with you?"

"Of course I do! I mean, if you want that. I won't be offended if you don't, I just thought—"

"I'm going to live with my brother!" she squealed, throwing her arms around him tight.

He hugged her back, squeezing hard, then nudged her toward me. Suddenly I had a face full of teenager.

"Can you believe it, Harlow?"

I barely contained my happy tears as I held her. "I'm so fucking glad you're getting out of that home, kiddo."

Lindsay and I had been trying to get her out since we turned eighteen, but never got anywhere because of our jobs and less-than-fantastic history in our own foster homes. But with Kylen being related by blood, it could finally happen.

I'd say it was fate if Hendrix hadn't turned the word into his version of a swear jar.

Addie grinned. "I'm still gonna be over every day, though, so don't go thinking the dog talk is over."

"Nope, you're Kylen's problem now."

Kylen smirked. "Not if I find a house big enough for all of us. Your place is cute, but I don't think Ranto and Hendrix will be willing to live apart from their mate and treasure for long. So if you're looking for somewhere, and I'm looking for somewhere..."

Bruin cleared his throat obnoxiously, leaning over to nibble at Kylen's neck as he growled against his skin. "I think you forgot someone."

"Did I? Oh, well, Lindsay would obviously be welcome, too." He yelped as Bruin gave a particularly hard nip. "Ow! Okay, you got me! Do you wanna move in?"

"Hm, I'd need space for my bike. But I'll consider it, since I like my roommates."

Addie stood, placing a freshly summoned daisy crown on Bruin's head. "I dub thee, King of the Dishes!"

He sighed but only to hide a smile. "Thanks, kid."

A piercing whistle snagged Addie's attention as Lindsay swaggered over from the building's entrance. "Hey! You ready for a movie with the OG big brother?"

"You're such a dork." Addie giggled, waving at us over her shoulder as she headed to the Camry with him. "See you guys later!"

Lindsay unlocked the car, grinning as he yelled, "Harls! I'm gonna stay with Kedron after I drop off Addie. Don't do anyone I wouldn't do!"

Sound advice, as always.

Harlow

As Kylen, Bruin, and I quietly climbed the stairs to my apartment, I felt their eyes on me, burning into my back. I knew Hendrix and Ranto would be in the apartment—most likely napping, in Ranto's case—but would this be an opportunity to have all of my lovers together? It felt selfish to even want it, but ever since I woke up from death in their arms, I've wanted to feel them surround me again. Only this time, under much more pleasurable circumstances.

The moment we entered the apartment, hands were on me. Bruin dragged my tank top up and over my head, kicking the door closed behind him, while Kylen pulled me in by my waist to kiss me deeply. I groaned, addicted to the sensation of his lips on mine, and tangled my fingers in his hair. He was the first of my lovers I trusted, but the only one I hadn't had inside me. This had been too long coming, and I was going to make sure it had been worth the wait.

A hard length pressed into me from behind, and my bra dropped from my shoulders before tattooed fingers cupped my breasts, then thumbs flicked over my piercings.

"Fuck, I'm obsessed with these." Bruin's voice was an erotic rumble in my ear.

I squirmed between them, my arousal pooling in my panties. Kylen's tongue massaged my own, tasting me and leaving me breathless.

"I hope this isn't a private party." Hendrix growled from the door to my bedroom.

Kylen released my mouth, and I dropped my head back on Bruin's shoulder to look over at my gryphon and raiju. Ranto leaned on the doorframe beside Hendrix, wearing nothing but adorable chicken nugget boxer briefs and a scrunchie holding his long hair up in a messy bun.

"We have the apartment to ourselves tonight." I murmured, reaching for Hendrix.

He crossed the tiny room in two strides, taking my hand and kissing my fingers, followed by my palm. No one in my life had ever cared for me the way he did. I loved how he treated me like something precious, literally his treasure.

"Excuse me, gentlemen."

In one swift movement, Hendrix sneaked an arm between me and Kylen and scooped me out of my witch-sandwich, hiking me over his shoulder with my ass in the air.

Kylen blinked at Bruin, then turned a scowl on Hendrix. "Did you just *yoink* our witch?"

"We're taking her to bed." The suggestion in his tone had everyone converging on the bedroom faster than I could say orgy.

He dropped me in the middle of the mattress and yanked off my sneakers and socks. "We'll take care of you, Treasure."

Ranto lay next to me, turning my head for a long kiss. He swallowed my moan of frustration as Hendrix dropped chaste kisses along the waistband of my jeans. The bed dipped on my other side, then a blonde head dipped to draw a warm, wet tongue over my pierced nipple. As Hendrix relieved me of my jeans, Kylen's hand drifted down my torso and sneaked under my panties to dip into my wetness.

"Mm, you're soaked," he whispered, biting my earlobe.

I whimpered as Ranto released my lips with a grin worthy of his wolf form. He rubbed his thumb over my bottom lip, watching me twitch as Kylen worked my core. "Who do you want to fuck you first, mate?"

I shuddered as Kylen's finger entered me, curling in just the right way that his name slipped out on a moan.

"Definitely didn't cheat there, did you?" Bruin snorted from the foot of the bed.

Kylen chuckled and added another finger. "Not at all. And even if I did, I call dibs."

Hendrix scoffed. "You can't call—"

"I'm the only one who hasn't seen our beautiful girl fall apart yet." He kissed my temple, stroking me more insistently. "So yeah, I call fucking *dibs*."

I nodded frantically, bucking my hips to get his fingers deeper as the heat pooling in my belly threatened to send me over the edge.

"In fact, I think I need a little preview." He worked me faster, thumbing my clit and sending warning sparks through me until fireworks exploded behind my eyelids.

My body bowed backward, the breath leaving me in a keening cry as I simultaneously tried to push him away and bring him closer.

"She's so gorgeous when she lets go like that..." Hendrix's awed murmur broke through the daze of my orgasm.

I desperately grasped for awareness as Kylen removed his fingers and pulled my panties down to my ankles. I didn't want to miss a moment of this.

"You'll get to see it again pretty soon. Oh, and, Bruin? Be a good boy and prep yourself. I'll still have plenty for you after I've claimed our girl."

A shiver of delight passed through me at the smug, yet commanding tone Kylen used, and I couldn't help but hope Bruin was equally turned on by it. I wanted my men happy, and if they found it together, I was all for it.

As each of them stripped off and I found myself surrounded by four hard cocks, everyone took a moment to reposition themselves. Ranto and Hendrix lounged beside the headboard, Bruin lay beside me on his stomach, and Kylen settled between my thighs, rocking his hips to drag his length along my slit.

"I need you inside me now. No more waiting."

At last, he notched his tip at my entrance and pushed into me with a long, hard thrust. As he bottomed out inside me, he took a moment to breathe, like he couldn't believe we'd made it here. Then, with a wicked smile, he drew almost all the way out and slammed back in, setting a brutal pace. A long moan left me as he sat back on his knees, but he wasn't going far. In a feat of strength I hadn't known him capable of, he hauled me into his lap, hitting me at a deeper angle that made my toes curl and my ability to use the English language limited. Taking a tight grip on my jaw, he slammed his lips to mine in a kiss that was all tongues and teeth and passion.

I raked my nails down his back, desperate to be as close to my nature witch as I could. To make him feel as out-of-control as he made me.

"Are you close, baby?" he asked, altering his pace so that he moved within me in agonizingly slow strokes.

A small whimper broke from me, and he lay me on my back, surging over me so that I could feel every inch of him dragging over my delicate flesh.

"I wanna feel you come around me, Harlow. Can you do that for me? Come again, and let us all watch you, beauty."

He reached between us to circle my clit, and I broke. He kept fucking me through my orgasm until he followed me into the abyss.

As we lay on our sides, catching our breath, I glanced up at the two men watching from the headboard.

"How'd I do for my first show?"

Hendrix snorted, "First? Treasure, you have no shame, and I adore that about you."

Ranto stroked himself lazily. "Ten out of ten. Though personally, I prefer those interactive shows, if you catch my drift."

"I think I do."

With a quick peck on the lips for Kylen, I crawled up the bed to sit on Ranto's lap. "Is this what you had in mind?"

"Close. Let me just..."

He motioned for me to rise with a hand, and as I lowered myself, he positioned his cock, so I impaled myself on it. His eyes fluttered closed, and I held onto his shoulders, my nipples pressed against his chest, as I ground down on him.

Working my hips, I built a slow, steady rhythm that had him hitting the deep parts of me perfectly, while teasing my clit with his pubic bone.

"I love when you take what you want, mate." He gasped, fingers digging into my hips hard enough to bruise. "Keep going, that's it. That's my mate."

His hips bucked up into my thrusts, and I quivered around him uncontrollably, tumbling through another orgasm and pulling him with me.

Before I could take a second to catch my breath, Hendrix's arms looped around my middle for the second time that night and positioned me on my knees in front of Bruin. "Ready, Treasure?"

I grinned, my arms shaking as I watched Kylen take up position behind my weather witch. "Not even a little."

Kylen leaned down over Bruin's back, licking up his neck, and said, "If you even think about coming before she does, you'll have so much more than vines to worry about."

Bruin's eyes widened, and he looked at Hendrix, "Do me a favor, big guy. Fuck her stupid. *Please.*"

Hendrix's low laugh rumbled along my back as he gripped my hips and slammed me onto his cock.

He drilled into me from behind, and I was dick-drunk, the noises coming from my throat something too explicit for Pornhub. Lucky for my ego, Bruin was in a similar situation. The room filled with the sounds of skin slapping skin and wanton moans. As the lines between my body and his began to blur, Hendrix's hand smacked down across my ass, making me clench around him with a strength I didn't know I had left in me.

"You like that, Treasure?" he asked, slapping the other cheek with just as much force, then moaning when I clenched again.

Fuck, I was unlocking so many kinks with these men, and we'd barely gotten started.

"Sounds like a yes. Now, I'm going to fill you with my cum, Treasure. And you better hold on to it until Bruin gets to you."

Ranto groaned in appreciation from his position at the end of the bed.

Oh Gods...

His fingers moved to my clit, and I barely held onto consciousness. These men were going to ruin me worse than a curse ever could.

Hendrix roared and pressed me into the mattress, pumping

his release into me as my inner muscles worked overtime. I was as melty as a good grilled cheese as Hendrix softly kissed down my spine to my abused pussy. He ran a finger gently through my swollen folds. "You did so well, Treasure."

I could have fucking purred.

He slapped my hip, encouraging me onto my back.

"Now be a good girl and spread your legs so the biker can kiss you all better."

Groans sounded all over the room, and I felt heat burn in my face until I saw the look of unbridled lust in Bruin's eyes.

"Get over here, Sparky."

Kylen pulled out of him long enough for them to reposition between my legs.

"I think if I have another orgasm, I might die... again."

"Well, I did promise to kill you."

My nature witch chose that moment to slam back into Bruin, and his deep groan ghosted over my flesh. My whole body felt hypersensitive, wrung out, and completely satiated. Bruin dragged his tongue up my slit, gathering Hendrix's release with a hum that sent chills through my body.

"Don't you fucking dare touch yourself." Kylen warned him. "You come hands free, or not at all."

Bruin huffed a laugh, flicking his tongue over my clit before spearing it inside me for a couple of lazy strokes.

"You say that like it's a threat, but I've been waiting for permission since Hendrix told me to eat his cum out of our girl."

Kylen cursed, his pace stuttering as he curled over Bruin's back.

Bruin continued to lap lazily at me, somehow knowing that I needed his attention more than another orgasm, and when Kylen had recovered his voice, he growled, "Come."

With a gasp, Bruin let go and streams of cum pumped on to

the sheets beneath us. As he caught his breath, he pressed a sweet kiss to my inner thigh.

"Love you, Sparky."

Gods, I loved these men. Each of them, in their own way. They fucking owned me, and I was more than fine with it because I owned them right back.

Fate had brought us together through a curse—even Hendrix couldn't deny it—but it was our choice to stay together.

Forever.

***

Thank you so much for reading!

That's it for Harlow and her men, we hope you enjoyed reading them as much as we enjoyed writing them!

If so, please consider leaving a review here

MAKE sure to turn the page to find out about the next installment in the Cursed Coven of Spells Hollow world!

WANT to find out what's coming up next for these authors?

Sign up for TL's newsletter here!

And Katherine's newsletter here!

UP NEXT...

Finding peace is hard when you're surrounded by the dead.

Morrigan has spent her childhood running from the ghost of people's past to appear normal and fit in, but her necromancy powers keep bringing her spirits who need closure.

Once upon a time, she found solace in taking care of the archives that were rarely visited by the living, but when an old family curse threatens her livelihood she knows she has to act.

Drawn back to Spells Hollow, Morrigan will have to listen to both the living and the dead to undo the curse and save her sanity.

Read Wallflower Witch today!

Wallflower
WITCH
THE CURSED COVEN OF SPELLS HOLLOW
RACHELLE BONIFAY
ROSEYK KLAYBORN

EXPLORE THE WITCHES OF SPELLS HOLLOW

Warrior Witch by TL Hamilton & Katherine Isaac
Wallflower Witch by Rachelle Bonifay & Roseyk Klayborn
Whimsical Witch by Emmy Dee & Whimsy Nimsy
Wicked Witch by Amber Nicole
Wandering Witch by KZ Merlin
Wishful Witch by Maya Black
Wildfire Witch by Ella Hendricks
Wayward Witch by Zoey Indiana
Wedded Witch by Crystal North

ALSO BY TL HAMILTON

M/F Sports Romance

The Perfect Stroke

Split - Kane & Darcy Pt 1

Shatter - Kane & Darcy Pt 2

Shock - Evie & Xavier

Fox Academy

Kicking it with the Winger

M/F Military Romantic Suspense

At All Costs

Target Me

Heal Me

Contemporary RH

Where in the world

Not with the band (coming soon)

Paranormal RH

Moon Dust Library/ Silver Springs Library Standalones

Moonlit Alexandrite

Moonlit Alexandrite: Crafty Seductions

Jewels Cafe: Jacinth

ALSO BY KATHERINE ISAAC

Contemporary RH

The Night Shift Before Christmas

Paranormal RH

Moon Dust Library

Moonlit Agate

Twisted Fate

ABOUT TL HAMILTON

Hi guys, I'm TL

I live in Melbourne, Australia, with my hubby, two little boys, Arlo the wonderful, and Hugo the turtle.

I love stories, and daydreaming about new stories, which is why I write all over the romance spectrum from romcom right through to the dark, gritty hold onto your seats drama.

I am happiest when the characters in my head are behaving.

Reviews are the life blood of indie authors, so if you read my work and enjoy it, please consider leaving a review in exchange for my everlasting adoration.

Come and join the fun in my reader group on Facebook

About Katherine Isaac

Katherine Isaac lives and works in Wales with her beloved cat-son. Growing up surrounded by mythology and history has fueled her love for epic stories of magic, mystery, and romance.

She is happiest with her nose in a book, pinned down by a cat, or surrounded by nature; whether that's lying on the grass or diving in the ocean.

Katherine describes herself as an eternally sleep-deprived pixie, with the mouth of a sailor and too many characters living in her brain.

ACKNOWLEDGMENTS

For the longest time, it felt like this book wasn't going to happen. The series kept getting pushed behind the scenes and there were so many setbacks. But Harlow is finally out in the world!

Therefore, our biggest thank you has to go to the readers who made us get this series going. You've embraced Harlow and her coven sisters, and gave us the determination to see this series through. THANK YOU!

We'd also like to extend huge thank you's to Katie for her fantastic edits, Jodie for the series' beautiful covers, Jamie for being the best alpha reader we could ask for, Susan for her historical knowledge and making sure we didn't say "this fucking guy, amirite?" in the diary entries, Andrea for her endless support, and Sam for being the series' biggest cheerleader. We love you all!

Thank you Emmy, our best frog, for simply being the ray of sunshine you've always been. Neither of us know where we would be without your love, rants, and A+ gif usage. We love you so much!!

Thank you Crystal, the final (and snuggliest) third of Nightshade Publishing. We never imagined this series would lead to us collaborating to create not just The Cursed Coven of

Spells Hollow, but organizing a Halloween charity anthology and working towards more shared worlds in the future. You're an inspiration to us and we can't wait to see what the future holds for Nightshade.

And as always, we couldn't do any of this without our family, friends, and most importantly, animal companions. We can't say "fur-babies" because unlike Katherine with her only-child cat, TL has an impressive variety of species living with her. She's basically a Disney princess. Now if only they did the dishes...

We can’t wait to see you all for our next collab!

shifty eyes

Drops smoke bomb

<3

Printed in Great Britain
by Amazon

46342798R00131